CHOICES

Candy land

written and directed by

SA'ID SALAAM

"They ask you about intoxicants and gambling. Say, 'In them is great sin and [yet, some] benefit for people. But their sin is greater than their benefit."

Qur'an(2:219):

Table of Contents

CHAPTER ONE:
New Year, New Me?

Desiree Carter stared into the bathroom mirror like she was trying to see the version of herself she swore was hiding somewhere behind the glass.

The toothbrush drooped from her lips, foam threatening to spill as she studied the face she'd grown tired of seeing. Brown skin kissed by undertones of gold. Wide-set eyes that always seemed to be searching for something—answers, maybe, or approval. Her thick curls sat piled in a lazy bun, the kind that said she'd tried but not too hard. Tiny gold studs winked under the flickering fluorescent light, like they were the only ones still confident about her reflection.

She tilted her head to the left, then the right.

Not ugly. Not pretty. Just regular.

Regular like kids nobody noticed until they disappeared.

"Junior year," she murmured around the toothpaste. The words came out like a promise to herself and a dare to the world. "Let's get it."

"Desiree! Time! Bus gonna leave you!" From outside the door, her mother's voice rang out—sharp, rhythmic, reliable. The sound bounced through the hallway, equal parts love and alarm clock. Evelyn Carter didn't believe in lateness or laziness.

"I'm coming!" Desiree called, spitting, rinsing, wiping her mouth, and giving herself one last glance. The girl in the mirror still looked regular, but there was a little more life behind her eyes. Enough to fake confidence for one more day.

She danced through her small bedroom, snatching up her denim jacket and stuffing a Pop-Tart into her bag. The smell of coffee and cocoa butter drifted through the air—a scent that was home, no matter how small or old the house felt. The hallway carpet swallowed her footsteps as she rushed down the stairs.

Her mother was in the kitchen, already dressed in scrubs, hair pulled into a bun that said she meant business. Her hospital badge hung at her chest like armor. Evelyn Carter was a nurse—steady hands, sore feet, no excuses. She'd seen too many people let life run them over and decided long ago she'd rather walk uphill every day than lie down in the road.

"You got everything?" she asked without looking up, her voice tight with the rhythm of routine.

"Yeah," Desiree said, half chewing, half mumbling, hoping that answer worked for everything her mom might mean.

Evelyn turned just enough to raise an eyebrow. "Lunch?"

Desiree smirked. "Got it."

"And a Pop-Tart is not breakfast."

"I know, Ma," she said, smiling around the edges of guilt. She'd already unwrapped it.

Her mother poured coffee, slow and steady. "You got your mind right?"

Desiree blinked, caught off guard by the question. That was her mom's version of a hug—checking her mental before she stepped into the world. "Yeah, I'm good."

7

Evelyn finally met her eyes. Those same hazel-green flecks that made lying impossible. "Don't let nobody pull you off your path," she said, voice soft but firm. "Remember who you are."

"I won't," Desiree promised. She didn't always know exactly who she was, but she knew her mother believed she could be somebody—and that was enough for now.

She kissed her on the cheek and slipped out the door, the cool morning air hitting her like a wake-up slap.

*****

The bus was already huffing at the corner when she jogged up, waving at the driver. Inside, chaos lived and breathed—fresh sneakers, Bluetooth speakers, gossip pinging louder than the music. She slid into a half-empty seat and pulled her hood up.

Desiree wasn't unpopular, just... in-between. Friendly enough to have friends, quiet enough to go unnoticed when she wanted. Her mom called it "balance." Her friends called it "boring."

The bus jerked forward, and she scrolled through the group chat. Notifications blew up her screen.

Tati: Y'all seen Malik's haircut??

Bree🐣: He got the summer fade but it's FALL, lmaooo.

🐥Jade: Issa new year. New rules. New bodies.

🐣Malik🐣: Y'all obsessed. lol.

🐥Jade: Desiree, where u at? Slide thru lunch table 6.

Desiree raised an eyebrow. Jade never hit her directly. They weren't enemies, just from different worlds. Jade was all lip gloss and loud laughs, the kind of girl who never waited for permission. Desiree was grades, quiet confidence, and the honor roll crew. Still, it felt nice to be noticed.

She looked out the window as the city rolled by—graffiti-tagged bus stops, corner stores opening early, kids she used to know standing in doorways like they'd already given up. She told herself she was different. She had plans. She had goals.

"You want it, you gotta work for it," her mother always said. Desiree repeated it under her breath like a prayer, like it could armor her from everything waiting outside those bus windows.

*****

By third period, the new-year buzz had faded into the usual hum of routine. Teachers preaching rules, phones sneaking under desks, someone snoring in the back already. Desiree tried to focus, but Jade's lunch invite kept replaying in her mind like a song hook she couldn't shake.

At lunch, her usual table—Tati and Cam—waited like home base. Safe. Predictable. But her feet had other plans.

"Dez! Over here!" Cam waved.

"Be right back!" she lied with a smile that even she didn't believe.

Table Six was louder, brighter, and smelled like weed and coconut body spray. Jade sat cross-legged on the chair like she owned it. Her nails glinted like weapons, and Malik sat next to her, tattoos fresh and arms stretched like he owned her. There was a spot open—one seat that felt like an invitation and a warning.

"You made it, girl," Jade grinned, eyes scanning her outfit like she was judging and approving at the same time. "Sit down. We was just talking about the party this weekend."

"I don' t really–" Desiree started, fumbling for an excuse she hadn' t planned.

"Girl, don' t say you don' t party," Jade cut her off, the queen talking to the peasant.

Desiree stammered, "I mean, my mom don' t really–"

"Then she don't gotta know." Jade shrugged as if deceiving your mom was normal.

The whole table laughed, not mean, just confident–like rules didn' t apply to them. Malik grinned and nodded her way, and the knot in her stomach loosened.

"Okay," Desiree said softly. The word surprised even her.

"See you then!" Jade said, already back to talking about Malik' s haircut.

Desiree poked at her tray, the room louder now, brighter somehow. Maybe it was the lights. Maybe it was her heartbeat. Maybe it was the thought that–for once–she might actually belong somewhere.

*****

That night, Desiree lay in bed staring at the ceiling fan. The room was quiet except for the low hum of the blades and the faint buzz of her phone lighting up on the nightstand.

Bree🥚: You coming to Malik' s Friday? Don' t be lame.

Jade: Bring a chill fit. And an open mind.

Desiree stared at the screen until the words blurred. She could almost hear her mother's voice echoing in her head—'Don't let nobody pull you off your path.'

But curiosity is a whisper that turns into a shove. It doesn't sound dangerous until it's too late.

She set the phone down, staring at the ceiling fan as it spun in slow hypnotic circles. Somewhere deep down, she felt that click—the one between curiosity and temptation. The kind that has killed plenty of cats and broken even more hearts.

She exhaled softly and whispered to herself, "New year, new me."

But she didn't yet know what that would mean.

CHAPTER TWO:
"Just One Hit"

Friday came too fast.

One minute Desiree was swearing she wasn't the type to go to some boy's house party. The next, she was standing in front of her closet like it was a pop quiz she hadn't studied for.

"I'm not ready!" she groaned, biting her thumbnail as she flipped through hangers. The clothes looked the same as always — nothing good enough to make her feel like them.

"What's a 'chill fit,' anyway?" she muttered to herself, tossing jeans onto her bed. She wanted to look like she belonged without trying too hard. That was the trick. The cool girls never looked like they tried.

After changing twice, then three times, she settled on ripped jeans and a cropped hoodie. Cute, but not extra. She brushed her curls into a high puff, added a touch of lip gloss, and stood in front of the mirror.

The girl looking back at her didn't look scared. Or so she hoped.

"You ready," she told her reflection. Then smiled, pouted, blew a kiss. She giggled — still half little girl — before her phone buzzed.

Tati ♡: You still coming over? Movie night!

Desiree's thumb hovered above the keyboard. Can't tonight. Rain check? she almost typed. But something about lying to Tati made her chest hurt, so she didn't type anything at all.

She just stared at the message until the screen dimmed. Old friends didn't always fit into new worlds.

Downstairs, she texted her mom – *headed to Jade's for a school project* – and waited for the reply. It came quick: 👍.

That was the kind of trust her mother gave – earned over years, now about to be bent for the first time. Evelyn was probably already in bed, half-asleep in her scrubs, worn out from saving strangers for twelve hours straight. Desiree told herself she wasn't lying, not really. She was just... choosing her own night.

A black car pulled up at the corner. Music thumped low through the windows. The doors opened to laughter, perfume, and smoke.

Jade leaned out from the passenger seat. "Ayy, there she go! Hop in!"

Inside was Bree and some dude Desiree didn't recognize – tall, golds flashing in his grin, one hand on the wheel like he owned the city.

"That's Dez?" he asked, half-smiling.

"Yeah, she cool," Jade said, motioning her in.

Desiree climbed in, trying to act like she'd done this before. Her heart was racing but her face stayed still. Bree handed her a cup – pink liquid with crushed ice and fruit slices floating on top.

"Taste that," Bree said. "It's good."

13

Desiree took a cautious sip. It burned going down, hot and sweet at the same time. She winced but didn't show it. Bree saw the flinch anyway and laughed.

"Welcome to the real world, girl."

Desiree swallowed again, the heat spreading through her chest. The music, the laughter, the smell of weed in the air — it all blurred into something that felt bigger than her. For the first time, she felt like she was on the edge of something grown.

Malik's apartment complex looked alive when they arrived — cars double parked, bass rumbling through walls, people spilling out onto balconies with cups raised. Desiree followed Jade through the front door, and the sound hit her like a wave.

The air was thick — weed smoke, cheap cologne, fried food. The lights were low, a single lamp with a red bulb painting everything the color of danger. Bodies moved in rhythm, shouting over the music, the smell of sweat and perfume mixing like heat.

Desiree's heart thudded so hard she could feel it in her ears.

"Come on, loosen up!" Jade shouted over the beat, handing her another cup.

"I'm good," Desiree said, her voice small in the noise.

Jade raised an eyebrow. "Don't be acting like a narc."

The word stung. Desiree took the cup and drank. It burned worse this time, but the laughter around her made her want to laugh too.

"That's what's up!" Jade grinned.

Desiree smiled, the warmth in her stomach blooming into her

cheeks. The music started to feel like it was inside her instead of around her. The crowd, the lights, the sound — everything moved together, a living thing that swallowed her whole.

She didn' t know when her cup was refilled. Or when she started dancing.

But at some point, she stopped worrying about how she looked and started feeling the beat.

Later, she found herself on the back porch. The air was cool, damp with smoke. A small group sat in a circle passing a blunt, their laughter softer out here, almost peaceful.

Malik leaned against the railing, exhaling a cloud into the night. The orange glow from the tip of the blunt flickered across his jaw. He looked older now, calmer than the chaos inside.

"You ever smoked?" he asked, offering it toward her.

Desiree hesitated. "No. I don' t really do that."

He smirked. "It ain' t that deep. Just weed. Better than stress. Better than school. Better than pretending."

The others laughed in agreement. Desiree watched the smoke twist upward, pale and pretty under the porch light.

"It' s just one hit," Malik said. His tone was easy — a dare wrapped in a smile.

"Hit, hit, hit!" the group chanted playfully, like kids at recess daring someone to jump.

Desiree thought about her mom' s face, about Tati' s text she hadn' t answered, about the perfect GPA that was supposed to be her ticket out. Then she looked at Malik — smooth, confident, unbothered − and wanted to feel that way too.

Her fingers trembled as she took it.

She stared at the blunt like it might reveal the future. Then she brought it to her lips and inhaled.

The smoke clawed at her throat, hot and dry. She coughed hard, eyes watering while the group laughed, but it wasn't cruel laughter − it was belonging.

"First-timer!" someone called, handing her a bottle of juice.

She took a sip, the sweetness cutting the burn. A strange calm spread through her limbs, like her body had been holding its breath all her life and finally exhaled.

The colors sharpened. The music softened. Even the stars looked closer.

She giggled, surprised by the sound of her own voice.

For the first time in a long time, Desiree didn't feel regular. She didn't feel invisible. She didn't even feel scared.

She just felt... good.

It was almost 2 a.m. when she finally made it home.

The house was dark except for the porch light her mother always left on − the silent prayer that her daughter would come back safe. Desiree tiptoed through the door, shoes in hand, the hallway spinning just enough to make her laugh.

In her room, she collapsed on her bed still dressed, her head buzzing, her heart floating somewhere between happy and numb. She scrolled through her phone.

Jade had posted a blurry selfie − arms around her, both of them smiling.

Tagged: @dezz.carter 😶🫧 she lit fr

Desiree stared at the screen. Her notifications were blowing up − flame emojis, "who dat?" comments, compliments from people who never noticed her before.

"Dang!" Desiree reeled, wide eyed with wonder. She felt a rush − not from the weed, but from being seen.

She smiled into the glow of her phone until her eyelids grew heavy. The room tilted softly, the ceiling spinning like the fan above it.

For the first time that year, she fell asleep smiling. Not because life was better. But because, for one night, she'd finally felt like she belonged.

And somewhere deep down, in the quiet between dreams, a new voice whispered to her − the kind that sounds like your own but isn't.

If it feels this good once⋯ imagine what twice feels like.

CHAPTER THREE:
Chasing Chill

The first time getting high took a lot — a dare, a smile from Malik, a table full of strangers turned friends.

The second time didn't take anything at all, now it was routine. After school, behind the bleachers, a blunt making rounds like a secret handshake.

"Hmmm." Jade hummed, holding the smoke in before passing it. "You gotta stop coughing like that, girl. You embarrassing us."

"Whatever," Desiree said, laughing. She took the blunt without hesitation this time, like she'd been born knowing how. The smoke filled her lungs and her mind went quiet — the kind of quiet she didn't know she'd been missing.

By now, she was officially "in."

People she barely knew before greeted her in the halls. Her phone buzzed with new followers and flame emojis. She started wearing lashes and tighter jeans, swapped her art club hoodie for cropped tops and confidence she didn't really feel.

Her Instagram bio even changed:

vibes > validation.

Except validation was exactly what she was chasing.

At home, she kept things smooth. Her mom was too tired to notice the small changes — the late nights, the hidden lighters, the smell of smoke that clung to her hoodie. Desiree made sure the dishes were done, her bed made, her grades "good enough."

The perfect camouflage.

By October, the buzz wasn't about being high — it was about feeling normal. Weed was no longer a thrill; it was balance. She'd light up to steady her hands before a test, to calm down after school, to fall asleep when her brain wouldn't shut up.

Her bag always carried a mini deodorant, gum, and body spray — her holy trinity of disguise. She was careful, but not careful enough. She knew she'd slipped when Mrs. Reaves handed back the Algebra II test. Face down, like mercy.

Still, the red 57% glared through the paper like blood through gauze. Desiree stared at it, the numbers swimming. She'd never failed anything before.

"You okay?" Tati whispered from the next seat. They hadn't talked much lately, but real friends could always feel when something was wrong.

"Just a bad day," Desiree muttered, covering the grade.

"You been having a lot of those," Tati said softly.

"I'm fine," Desiree shot back too quick. She forced a smile, but her eyes told the truth.

Because she wasn't fine. Her thoughts jumped like skipping rocks. Her focus had holes in it. Her motivation sagged. What was the point of trying so hard if she already knew the ending?

Friday came with another party. Another chance to forget.

This one was smaller, darker. The music louder, the liquor cheaper. Desiree drank what someone handed her − clear, bitter, burning. They called it "white girl vodka." She laughed at the name, swallowed it anyway.

The night blurred fast − a flash of lights, the smell of smoke, the heat of bodies pressed too close. She danced until she couldn't tell if the beat came from the speakers or her chest. Malik found her in the kitchen, leaning against the counter with that lazy grin that made girls forget sense.

"There she go," he said.

"There you go," she teased back, her words slow, melted.

He laughed, leaning closer. His cologne was cheap but strong, his smile easy. When his hand brushed her back, she didn't move away. When he kissed her, she didn't stop him.

And when she woke up the next morning in Jade's guest room, fully dressed but not fully sure how she got there, she didn't ask. She just stared at the ceiling, head pounding, mouth dry. Her phone buzzed.

12 missed calls: MOM.

3 texts: TATI − "You good? You ain't answer none of my calls. Just don't forget who really care about you."

Desiree groaned, turned her phone face-down, and reached for the half-smoked blunt in the ashtray. One hit later, the guilt faded like fog.

"I'm good," she whispered to herself − the lie tasting better than the truth.

When she finally got home, her mom was waiting. Evelyn

stood at the counter, arms folded, uniform still on, face calm but tired.

"Stayed at Jade's?" she asked.

"Yeah," Desiree said, like it was nothing.

"And that's that, huh?" her mom said, no smile behind it.

"Ma, I done spent nights out before." she reminded.

"Yeah, at Tati's. I don't even know this Jade." Evelyn's tone softened, worry sneaking through the cracks. "I just hope you know what you're doing."

"I'm just doing me," Desiree said — and the truth was, she didn't even know who "me" was anymore.

"I see," her mother sighed. She wanted to argue but swallowed it. Fussing wouldn't fix it.

Back at school, the slide got steeper. Her drawings lost detail. Her essays lost focus. Her teachers noticed the distance behind her eyes.

"You have so much talent," her English teacher said one afternoon, handing back a half-finished paper. "Don't throw it away."

"I'm fine," Desiree lied again. But her voice cracked on the "fine."

After class, Malik was waiting outside. He had that look — the kind that always came with trouble.

"Got something new," he said, pulling a small pack of

colorful gummies from his pocket. "Edibles. Smoother. Better than smoke."

Desiree eyed them like they were candy, which they were – the wrong kind.

"I don't know…" she frowned.

"You trust me, right?" he said, leaning close.

She hesitated. She'd trusted him before, with laughs, with secrets, with pieces of herself she didn't get back.

Her head nodded anyway. "Yeah."

She took one. Popped it in her mouth. Chewed. Swallowed.

"What's it gonna do?" she asked.

"Make you feel like Silver Surfer riding clouds," he said, grinning.

He wasn't lying. Within the hour, her body felt weightless. Her thoughts melted like wax. The world slowed to a hum. She lay in bed later that night, staring at the ceiling fan as it spun, soft and hypnotic. Her limbs floated. Her heartbeat sounded far away.

No dreams came. Just stillness.

And for the first time, she didn't miss dreaming.

Days blurred into weeks. Highs blurred into habits.

Desiree didn't know it yet, but that was the night she stopped chasing fun and started chasing chill.

And chill, as she was about to learn, costs more than any party could ever give.

CHAPTER FOUR:
Bottom Shelf Dreams

"Tuh," Desiree huffed at her reflection and angled the mirror away. Lately, she studied everything except her own face – the chipped paint on the doorframe, the loose thread on her hoodie, the fog on the bathroom glass. Anything but the eyes that looked a little dimmer each week.

It wasn't that she'd stopped being pretty. The curls were still thick, the skin still smooth, the mouth still soft. But behind the eyes, the wattage had dropped. Like a bulb that used to light the whole room now flickered when the AC kicked on.

She told herself it was nothing. A phase. Stress. Junior year was heavy; everybody said that.She popped open her bag, found the last gummy tucked beside her lip gloss, and slid it under her tongue.

"I know what I need," she whispered, and waited for the edges of the day to blur.

*****

Her mother knew before she did. Mothers always do; nurses especially.

Evelyn Carter took in the evidence the way she charted vitals – small numbers turning into patterns: the dullness around the mouth, the lost appetite, the hoarse voice from laughing too hard in rooms that smelled like smoke. Papers turned in late. The way Desiree waited for the shower to run loud before she cracked her window and leaned out.

She held her tongue until she couldn't.

"You been off lately," Evelyn said one evening, folding warm towels on the couch while the local news murmured about storms and budgets and a teenager gone missing three neighborhoods over. "Grades slipping. You barely eat. You stay in that room with the door closed like it pays rent."

"I'm fine," Desiree said without looking up from her phone. It was her least favorite lie and the one she told most often.

"I know something's wrong, baby. I can feel it." Evelyn set the towel down and studied the side of her daughter's face.

"Ma, I just got a lot on my mind." Her tone sharpened because fear always hides behind attitude. "I'm not a baby."

"Is it a boy?" Evelyn asked gently; that's when most daughters switch lanes on their mothers.

"No." Desiree rolled her eyes. Malik's smile flashed in her head, then disappeared. She swallowed.

Evelyn's voice lowered. "You using something?"

"What? No!" The word jumped out too fast. Her chest squeezed. She kept her face still, hands still, anything still.

"I'm not stupid," Evelyn said. "I'm a nurse."

"I said I'm fine." Desiree stood like she could walk away from the conversation, from the house, from herself.

"Can't be fine talking to me like that," her mother snapped back, standing too. The standoff held for one heartbeat, then two, until Desiree sank onto the couch again.

24

"My bad, Ma," she whispered, staring at the TV without hearing it.

"I'm saying slow down. Don't rush to be grown. Ain't nothing out there but bills and funerals." Evelyn's voice broke and she caught it, cleared her throat, smoothed a towel that was already smooth. "I see kids all night in that ER who grew up too fast. Some become mothers before they become women. Some don't become anything because something becomes them."

"I'm good," Desiree said, and fled before the tears could catch up.

*****

Jade posted a video that night riding shotgun in a Scat Pack, braids whipping the air, nails glinting like sign language for "look at me." Desiree watched twice, then a third time, then tossed her phone onto the bed like it had said something slick.

She lit a blunt at the cracked window. Inhale, hold, exhale out into the alley so the house didn't keep the secret. The first two pulls didn't touch her; the third softened her shoulders and the knot behind her eyes.

Her thumbs moved on their own.

What you doing

Slide thru. Just me and you.

On my way.

She didn't ask for permission; permission came with questions. The hallway creaked. The front door clicked. She was moving before fear could put its shoes on. Before reason could reason she was out the door.

*****

Malik's building used to be a decent brownstone, split into too many apartments by someone with quick hands and a dull saw. The hallway smelled like old carpet and someone's dinner. A TV blared behind a door while a baby cried behind another. Desiree knocked with her knuckles tucked like she knew what she was doing.

He opened shirtless, hair twisted, eyes half-lidded from something that didn't come in a bottle. He smiled easy and stepped back to let her in.

"You good?" he asked, brushing a curl off her cheek the way boys do when they want to be remembered.

"Not really. Me and my moms," she sighed, letting the words sit between them so she wouldn't have to.

"I got something for that." He reached behind the couch and came up with a bottle that used to have a label. The liquid inside was the color of bad decisions. He poured two small cups and slid one to her.

"What is it?" she asked without fear. Fear can be good, especially when it came to bottles with no label.

"A lil' something," he said, and that had always been enough for her. One sip turned into two. Two turned into warm shoulders and slower thoughts.

"Relax," Malik murmured as his thumbs found her traps. "You too tense."

She let herself be arranged. Let quiet fill the places words should've gone. Let the liquor round off the corners of everything sharp.

*****

She woke alone in his bed, the morning gray, her hoodie inside out, mouth tasting like pennies. The sounds of a pan and a fork came from the kitchen. She blinked three times and waited for the part where last night snapped into place. It didn't.

"Malik?" Her voice surprised her − small and polite, like she was a guest in her own life.

He was shirtless at the stove, making eggs, no big deal. Nothing needed to be said because something had already been decided without words. He handed her a plate like they'd done this before, like they'd do it again.

They ate quietly, laughing once about some silly thing on his phone, two strangers performing a skit about being grown.

On the walk home the sky looked like a bad mood. She practiced explanations in her head: Phone died. Lost track of time. Jade's couch. We fell asleep watching a movie. Each sounded thin from the inside.

At the door, she hoped her mother would be gone. She was. Desiree slept in her clothes with the blinds half-open, sunlight cutting her face into stripes.

That afternoon, Evelyn cooked like she was kneading peace into the food. Desiree braced herself for a sermon; it didn't come. Sometimes silence is heavier than a belt. They ate. They talked about nothing. Desiree chewed each bite like it was proof she was still here.

*****

The weeks sped up. Desiree bent the parts of life that could bend and avoided the parts that couldn't.

First-period became optional. Homework turned into tomorrow-work. She pressed the snooze on everything except the high. She told herself she was balancing. She told herself she could stop. She told herself so many things she would've laughed at last year. Then Malik leveled her up.

"Got something new," he said behind the courts after school, like a man lifting a curtain. A white tablet sat on his tongue, then disappeared. He held another between two fingers and tapped her wrist, a magician asking for a volunteer.

"What is that?" Desiree asked.

"Percs." Malik replied nonchalantly. The word felt clean and clinical. Like a doctor would say it with a straight face. He didn't offer it to her palm; she stuck out her tongue because she wanted to be brave about the wrong thing. He placed it there like communion.

"What it do?" she asked – wrong order, too late.

"Like weed but better." He smiled because lies always sound true on a sunny afternoon.

He wasn't lying about the feeling. It rolled over her slow – a warm, tidal hush that padded her bones and put pillows around her thoughts. The angry clock in her chest stopped ticking. The world lost its hard edges. Even the part of her that watched herself make bad choices took a nap.

By dinner it had faded, but the memory of the quiet stayed bright. The next day, one pill was a treat. Then one-a-day was maintenance. Then maintenance looked like two. Some lines are brick walls. Others are chalk on the sidewalk that rain takes care of. She had stepped over without noticing she was on the other side.

*****

"Here go your girl," Bree sneered one morning, loud enough for Desiree to hear while pretending she couldn't. Groups rearrange quickly when one person changes weight. Bree's laugh had more bite these days; Desiree could tell whose house she'd been at by the color of her tongue.

Tati waited for her at the locker they'd shared side-by-side since sixth grade. Her face was calm but her hands told the truth, wringing the edge of her notebook.

"Dez, I don't know what's going on, but this ain't you." she grimaced like whatever it was stunk.

"You don't even know me anymore," Desiree said, and regretted it as soon as it left her mouth.

"I knew the you who stayed up drawing until your pencil ran out of lead. The you who made me playlists and cried at cartoons." Tati's voice wasn't angry; that made it worse. "I don't know this version."

"Then stop looking for her," Desiree said, softer now, because she was talking to herself too.

She caught Malik's name lighting up her screen and felt relief and dread at the same time. He wasn't texting to ask about her day. He wanted to know if she had any money.

Money lived in her mother's purse. Not much of it; a nurse's money is made of miles and overtime. Desiree stared at the leather bag on the dresser like it might call the police. She took a twenty with hands that didn't even shake.

First time. It wouldn't be the last. She told herself she'd pay it back. She told herself a lot of things.

*****

Art had always been the place she went when the words wouldn' t line up. Lately, the paper looked at her like do something, and her hand forgot how. She' d sharpen a pencil to a dagger and hover it above the page until the tip dulled from air.

Her sketchbook stayed closed so long the elastic left a groove in the cover. When she did force it open, what came out was messy — heavy shadows, hands without wrists, faces with eyes scratched out.

"Artists gotta make to feel regular," she told herself, and tucked the book away because she didn' t want to know what the new drawings meant. The pills didn' t make her great. They just made her not care she wasn' t.

*****

"Ho-hum," Desiree said out loud scrolling past Jade' s newest stunt — filtered night, filtered life, a caption about haters who weren' t actually hating. Desiree thought about texting Tati but pride is loud. She lit up instead. The smoke hit thin; tolerance is a math problem that always grows.

Malik texted pull up and she went because saying no is a muscle you have to lift early, and hers had atrophied.

His apartment smelled like cinnamon and something beneath it — the kind of chemical note you don' t notice until it stains your throat. A candle burned low, drowning in its own wax. The couch leaned. He looked tired in a way you can' t nap away.

"Crazy day?" she asked.

"Always." He poured from the bottle with the blank label. Two cups. Two reasons. "This help."

It helped — in the way that throwing a blanket over a mess

helps. You can't see the mess, but it's still right there.

"Relax," he said again, and the thing about hearing the same line is you start playing your part on cue. She let him rub circles into her shoulders; she let the room glide; she let the part of her that asked questions clock out early.

Evelyn saw the routine and swallowed the scream. Lectures had bounced off; this needed a plan, not a performance. She started Googling programs on her lunch breaks and whispered prayers on her way to work, the kind you don't say out loud because names make things real.

*****

Time sped up. Desiree learned the quiet ways people give up on you: teachers stop calling home; friends stop inviting you; the girl at the corner store stops carding because you've bought enough wrappers to be a regular. Desiree learned the quiet ways you give up on yourself: you stop counting days; you stop opening the portal; you stop opening the sketchbook.

"Yo," Malik said one afternoon, like a boy and a salesman at once. "You got me?"

She did. Twenty in ones from a pawned pair of earrings that used to belong to her mother and used to be a gift from her father. The cashier barely looked up. The guilt didn't either.

"Last time," she told the mirror that night.

"No, it's not..." The mirror blinked and told the truth back. Mirrors always tell the truth.

*****

Two weeks later, the pills started tasting different. She couldn't name it, but her tongue knew. They hit faster and

31

nastier; they dropped her further; they left a buzz in her teeth like a small, mean electricity.

"Strong batch," someone said with half a grin and half a warning. Desiree swallowed anyway. The first lesson of addiction is you always think you're the exception. The second is you're not.

She'd wake up sometimes not knowing the middle of the story, only the ending: a bathroom she hadn't planned to see, a bruise she couldn't explain, a text thread she didn't remember starting. She laughed those off the way kids laugh off falling in the hallway — too loud, too bright, too quick.

Nights ended under a bridge once, the sky huge and indifferent, the concrete humming with traffic. She thought about the fourth-grade sunflower that won a ribbon. She thought about her mother's hands. She thought about nothing, because nothing is easier than everything.

And then she went home because home stayed open. Evelyn left the porch light on like a lighthouse. She pretended not to notice the way Desiree walked, the slump, the flinch at brightness. She made eggs. She made soup. She made eye contact when she could catch it.

"I'm okay," Desiree said one morning, and for once her voice sounded like a question.

"I know," Evelyn said, and meant I know you're not. She kissed her hair like she did when Desiree was five and scared of thunder. "We gon' get you right."

Desiree nodded because nodding is free.

*****

The day Ms. Reaves emailed home, it wasn't about a

32

missing assignment. The subject line said Conference. The message said concern three different ways. Evelyn read it on her phone in the break room and stared through the vending machine until a coworker said her name twice.

That night she didn' t start a fight. She made a plan. And because she was a mother, she also made spaghetti.

"Hey," she said after dinner, wiping her hands on a towel. "I found a program. Short-term. Good reviews."

"I don' t need rehab," Desiree said, a laugh stuck to the end of the sentence like gum on a shoe. "I just need some sleep."

"You need help," Evelyn said softly. "Real help."

She didn' t make it a threat. She made it a promise. Desiree' s jaw worked. The part of her that wanted to be saved and the part that wanted to stay floating squared up inside her chest. It only took a second to decide which one would talk.

"I' m good," she said, channeling the girl who used to say it and mean it. Evelyn looked at her baby − taller now, tired now, still hers. She nodded once.

"Pack a bag." she ordered. Desiree laughed like that was cute but Evelyn didn' t laugh back.

The house got quiet except for zippers and the washing machine and a mother saying a prayer in a whisper she' d never used before.

*****

They admitted Desiree on a rainy Thursday. The intake nurse had forearms like tree trunks and a smile that didn' t move her eyes. The hallways smelled like disinfectant and lemon. The art on the walls looked like somebody's feelings on copy paper.

"You can cuss, cry, or be quiet," the night tech said with a shrug. "Just don't break nothing."

Desiree broke a chair by accident and a picture on purpose. She slept without sleeping, skin buzzing, brain sprinting in place. She blamed her mother. She blamed Malik. She blamed Jade. She blamed everybody but the girl in the mirror because mirrors don't argue back.

Somewhere around 4 a.m., the storm outside softened and the one inside her did too. She stared at the dark until her breaths lined up.

"I don't want this," she whispered to the ceiling that didn't care. "I just don't know how not to want it."

Morning didn't answer. Morning just arrived.

*****

Outpatient came next – three days a week, two hours a day in a room with a coffee maker that burned everything it touched. The videos were old; the worksheets were worse. People twice her age talked about losing houses, spouses, and teeth. Desiree felt wildly out of place and exactly in the right room.

"These folks are junkies," she thought, mean because she was scared. Then she remembered the window, the mirror, the twenty from her mother's purse. "Maybe I am too," she thought, and the honesty hurt less than she expected.

A counselor named Ms. Lena started clocking her. Middle-aged, warm voice, stern eyes. She didn't try to be cool; she tried to be kind. It worked.

"You're not broken, Desiree," she said after group one day, pausing in the doorway like she had all the time in the world. "You're hurting. Hurt people make hurt choices."

Desiree stared at the carpet until it blurred. Ms. Lena didn't fill the silence. She let it sit beside them like a third person.

"You ever look in the mirror and not know who you looking at?" the counselor asked finally.

"Every day," Desiree said, and her throat tightened around the words like they were too big to fit.

"Good." Ms. Lena smiled. "Means the old you still in there. She ain't gone; she hiding."

"She scared." Desiree admitted and blinked hard to keep the tears inside her eyes.

"Then we gon' help her." Ms. Lena tapped the table once like a gavel. "One choice at a time."

"Okay," Desiree whispered. Then louder. "Okay."

That night she stood in front of the mirror and forced herself to look. Not the hair, not the hoodie, not the lip gloss. The eyes. They were tired, yes, and sad, yes – but alive. She pressed her fingers to the glass like she could touch the girl underneath.

"I miss you," she told her reflection. The mirror told the truth back. It always does.

*****

The next afternoon, Desiree walked past a corner where a boy with a backpack sold amnesia by the pill. Her feet slowed; her chest hurt. She kept moving. Her phone buzzed.

Malik: Pull up?

She typed No and deleted it. Typed Busy and deleted that too. In the end she sent nothing and put the phone on airplane mode like she was flying somewhere else. For a few days, she did.

She ate. She slept on schedule. She cracked the sketchbook and drew a set of hands holding a smaller pair, both sets scarred, both sets steady. It wasn't brilliant. It was honest. She pinned the page to her wall and stared until she felt the urge to tear it down pass.

Then came the text that always comes.

You up?

You good?

Got something clean. Better.

She held the phone like it might burn her. Maybe it already had. Desiree looked at the drawing again and felt the smallest click of something inside line up true.

Not today, she told herself. Not now.

And for that day — just that day — she was right. She didn't know new storms were forming two blocks away with pills that looked like the old ones but weren't. She didn't know bridges could have basements. She didn't know how much a body can survive until it can't.

What she knew was this: the quiet she wanted didn't live in a bottle or a baggie. The quiet she wanted lived in the space between a choice and the next breath.

CHAPTER FIVE:
Mirrors

"This girl do not know how to return stuff," Desiree muttered, flipping pillows and tugging on a tangled phone cord like it owed her money. She wasn't really mad; searching was a habit now — for a charger, for a lighter, for the feeling that used to live inside her chest before everything got noisy.

Her room had that lived-in chaos she pretended meant creativity: clothes draped like tired people, sketchbook closed with the elastic biting a groove across its cover, a half-empty bottle of body spray keeping secrets near the window. She was on her knees when she saw it — the small plastic bag tucked behind the jewelry box.

At first, her brain said candy. Her nose told the truth before she could lie to herself. Bitter. Chalky. The kind of smell that turns your mouth to dust just from looking.

Her heart hiccuped. She knew exactly where it came from and exactly what it meant. That was the thing about choices: you can pretend you tripped, but you remember lifting your foot.

She scooped the bag up, turned it once in the light, then slid it back like she could rewind time if her fingers were gentle. The mirror over her dresser caught her in the act. She didn't linger. Mirrors tell the truth and don't even say it nice. Down the hall, a drawer closed followed by a cabinet closing, then footsteps.

"Desiree!" her mother called, voice too even. "Come here a minute."

A minute is only sixty seconds until your body starts counting in years. Evelyn was at the kitchen table with a stack of folded laundry like armor. The plastic bag sat on top of a white T-shirt as if it belonged to the house, as if it paid rent.

"What is this?" her mother asked, and didn't blink.

"It's not mine." she blurted. The lie tasted like pennies. She swallowed anyway.

"You really think I'm stupid?" Evelyn's voice didn't rise; it got heavy. "I ran the number on those pills." She tapped the bag with one finger, a nurse at work. "This ain't cough drops."

"It's just—" Desiree started, then aborted the sentence midair. Just nothing.

"You know how many kids don't make it to see their mamas again behind 'just'?" Evelyn asked. "You bringing this poison in my house?"

"It's not⋯" Desiree tried again. Her throat was the size of a pinhole. Shame and anger elbowed each other in a small room inside her chest. "I'm right here. I'm fine."

"You could be not." Evelyn's hands shook and she trapped them in her lap. "One wrong pill, one time."

"I got it under control." Desiree looked at the floor. Counting tiles felt easier than counting losses.

"And I'm the Queen of England," her mother said softly. The softness was worse than yelling. "Go to your room. We'll talk in the morning."

"Okay," Desiree said, because there was no other word. She turned and walked down the hall, pulse thrumming in her ears like music from somebody else's party.

She sat on the edge of her bed and stared at the mirror. Her face looked like a wanted poster for a girl she used to be. Sleep would not come and the walls were loud. The window latch was louder.

She stood up quietly and donned her shoes even quieter. Backpack slid on smoothly and the front door a whisper.

*****

Jade's house was loud the way neglect is loud – not volume, but clutter that makes noise just by existing. Too many bodies for too little space. Fast food bags stacked like décor. A TV talking to itself in an empty room.

"Hey girl!" Jade sang, eyeliner smudged into a permanent decision. "Come in."

Desiree stepped over a pair of toddler sneakers and a teenager asleep on a mattress with no sheet. The air smelled like menthol, grease, and sweet rot beneath it all. She wanted to gag and wanted not to care. The second want was stronger.

"You got anything?" she asked, straight to the point. Her voice didn't sound like hers; it sounded like a voice that understood how to open doors.

"You know I do," Jade said, laughing at the obvious. She reached into her bra and came back with a bag of light-blue pills. "Robbie blessed me."

"Thank you," Desiree said, and meant it too much. She dry-swallowed one. It lodged in her throat like a hard truth. She forced it down, waited.

The buzz came as a gentle thief – stole the corners first, rounded the room, padded the edges of thought. Relief arrived like an apology she'd been waiting for that no one owed her.

She slept on a couch whose cushions had given up. Woke to noise and neon, swallowed again. Woke to hunger and guilt, swallowed again.

Days that should've had names passed without raising their hands.

*****

When Desiree finally came home, it was 2 a.m. The porch light hit her like a spotlight. She blinked into it, a deer who knew better.

The door opened before she could knock. Evelyn stood there in scrubs, face the color of not-sleeping. She said nothing, stepped back, pointed at the bathroom.

"Shower. Pack your things." she demanded like she rarely did.

"What?" The word came out with a laugh attached, like a reflex. "Ma–"

"Pack. Your. Things." Each period was a full stop. "You need help. Real help."

"I just needed some air," Desiree said. It sounded small, even to her. "I'm fine now."

"You're not dying under my roof." Evelyn's voice cracked on dying and came back iron. "Not on my watch."

That broke something old and stubborn in Desiree. The fight

deflated. She nodded and did as she was told because she didn't trust the part of herself that wanted to argue.

She showered until the water went from warm to warning. Steam blurred the mirror until her face didn't exist, and that felt like peace.

She threw clothes into a bag with no plan except go.

*****

Intake smelled like lemon cleaner and loneliness. A poster on the wall said Today is a new day in cheerful font that had never seen a relapse. The night tech had braids and soft shoes and a look that said she'd met a thousand Desires and learned them all by first name.

"You can cuss, cry, or sleep," she told Desiree, sliding a clipboard across the counter. "Just don't break nothing."

"I'm not breaking anything," Desiree said, then knocked a plastic chair over with her backpack two minutes later.

They catalogued her: phone in a Ziploc, shoelaces gone, feelings off. Her room had a window that didn't open, a bed that squeaked any time breath happened, and a desk built to hold a pencil and a prayer.

The quiet at 3 a.m. is not kind. It lists your recent history without commentary. Desiree tried to stare the ceiling down; the ceiling did not blink.

"I don't want this," she whispered. She wasn't sure if she meant the room, the life, or the ache. "I just don't know how to not want it."

Her body didn't sleep. It shut off and turned on in intervals, like a machine trying to remember its settings.

Morning came because it always does. People shuffled into a room with coffee that tasted like punishment. A counselor with a calm voice and worried eyebrows said the words disease and choice and community. Desiree doodled in the margins of a handout until the paper tore.

In group, a woman with a wedding ring and raw knuckles talked about selling the ring before the knuckles. A man with Sunday-school eyes described dying twice in a McDonald's bathroom and the third time being the charm. Desiree listened hard and tried to decide if she was like them. The answer moved every time she reached for it.

After, a counselor – not young, not old, brown skin with a map of smile lines – stopped her at the door.

"You're not broken, baby," she said, fast like she knew Desiree might run. "You hurting. Hurt people make hurt choices. We gon' teach you new ones."

Desiree nodded without meaning to. The words fit. They did not fix.

*****

She went home after the first round like you do when you follow all the rules and hope rules are enough. Outpatient started. Three afternoons a week in a room where feelings were stapled to worksheets. Desiree showed up, breathed, spoke when picked, said the lines that sounded good and sometimes were true.

For a while, she did the small things that add up: ate, slept, turned the phone off when a certain name lit the screen. She even opened the sketchbook. Drew a pair of hands holding a smaller pair – both scarred, both steady. Taped it to the wall where the light hit first thing. Then the world wobbled, like a table with one short leg.

She was walking home when she saw a boy at the end of the block — backpack slung low, mouth bored, eyes doing math. He slipped something to a girl who looked like a before picture and walked on. Desiree felt the chemical memory light up along her gums like a cruel smile.

Her phone buzzed.

You up?

Another ping.

Clean batch. Promise.

She set the phone face-down on her dresser and looked in the mirror. The girl there looked like she wanted to be believed. She looked like she deserved it. She also looked like somebody who couldn't stand one more bad decision.

"Not today," Desiree told the mirror. The mirror didn't clap. It held.

*****

Two days later, temptation came in a nicer outfit. Not a boy on a corner, not a text with a lie. Curiosity with lip gloss on. It started with boredom, graduated to restlessness, put on a jacket and called itself errands.

She walked past the train station, past the place where the air always smelled like bleach and old rain. Her feet remembered a bathroom tile that had once felt like goodbye. She kept walking and didn't know if that made her brave or lucky. At home, Evelyn was folding towels again like a meditation.

"How was group?" she asked, like she was asking about

weather, like both could turn ugly without warning.

"Fine," Desiree said, which meant I stayed and didn't bolt and that counts.

Evelyn nodded. They didn't overtalk it. Too many words wear hope out. They ate spaghetti. Laughed at a dumb commercial. Watched a game neither of them cared about because the noise felt like protection. Later, in bed, Desiree stared at the ceiling until it blurred into sky. She pictured a future that didn't require anesthesia to enter.

She fell asleep holding that picture like a ticket.

*****

The next morning she woke up hungry for the first time in a long time. Toast. Egg. Tea. Her mother smiled at the plate like it was a diploma.

"You look like yourself today," Evelyn said, and meant it like a blessing.

"Trying," Desiree said with her mouth full, which was its own kind of prayer. Her phone stayed quiet. The city did not. Sirens did what sirens do. A helicopter drew circles only God could see. Somewhere, a car door slammed like a period at the end of a name.

Desiree opened the sketchbook and drew a mirror facing a window – each reflecting the other's light. It wasn't brilliant. It was honest. That felt like enough for now. She taped the drawing next to the hands. Two truths in a row. Then she sat on the edge of her bed and looked up. The mirror gave her back a face she recognized, not all the way, but more than yesterday.

"Hey," she told the girl. "I'm gonna keep choosing you."

The girl didn't speak. She didn't have to. The promise lived in the room, quiet and stubborn. Outside, the porch light clicked off. Inside, morning did what morning does – turned possibility into hours, one after the other, ready to be spent.

CHAPTER SIX:
Crossroads

Desiree always thought recovery meant moving forward – one step, one day, one choice.

No one told her it could also mean standing still.

Weeks passed as slow amolasses. Like a remake of the movie Groundhog Day, except it was group, home, workbooks, home again. Same hallway, same window, same view of a world she wasn't sure she wanted to rejoin.

The noise of her old life was gone, but so was the color. She missed the hum of chaos – the fake confidence, the dizzy highs, even the danger. Because even danger meant feeling.

Now, sobriety was like holding your breath in a room full of air.

*****

On a Thursday afternoon, she sat on the edge of her bed scrolling through old pictures. Her feed was a museum of masks: smoky eyes, red cups, laughter that looked too wide for her face.

Each image came with ghosts – people who no longer texted, parties that had turned into problems, friends that had become footnotes. She hovered over "delete."

Didn't press it. Couldn't. Erasing proof meant admitting how lost she'd been.

Her phone buzzed.

Tati ♡: U coming to art show tomorrow? Ms. Reaves said you should.

Tati ♡: She still believe in you, girl. So do I.

Desiree's first instinct was to say no. Crowds still made her skin crawl. But the idea of being seen — for something other than failure — tugged at her.

She typed:

I'll try.

*****

The next day smelled like spring pretending to start early. She put on jeans that actually fit, a denim jacket that made her feel almost confident, and tied her curls up high — not perfect, but hers. The bus ride felt foreign, but familiar in the bones. Kids laughed, phones blared, life went on like it hadn't paused for her detour.

At school, eyes found her — some curious, some cautious, some pretending not to look. She felt every one of them.

"Dez!" Tati waved from across the hall, grinning like the past hadn't happened. They hugged tight — no questions, no explanations, just a moment of home.

"You look good," Tati said. "Like… good-good."

"Don't gas me." Desiree laughed.

"I'm serious. I missed you." her friend vowed. It wasn't forgiveness, but it was close enough.

The art show was smaller than she remembered – a few easels, some folding tables, snacks that went untouched. Still, the room buzzed with quiet pride.

She walked the perimeter slow, eyes scanning landscapes, portraits, pencil sketches – some shaky, some stunning. And then she saw it: a charcoal drawing of two hands clasped together, scarred but steady.

Her drawing.

Ms. Reaves had framed it. Underneath the frame, a small placard read:

"Resilience" – by Desiree Carter.

Her chest tightened. For a moment she forgot how to breathe. People were stopping to look at her work – not her mistakes, not her mugshot in the whispers, not her name in rumor. Her art.

"Thought you'd skip it," Ms. Reaves said, appearing beside her, arms crossed in that familiar mix of pride and tough love.

"I almost did." she admitted.

"But you didn't. That's growth." the woman smiled. Desiree swallowed and picked her words.

"I didn't think I deserved to be here." she decided.

"That's the thing about art. It don't ask if you deserve it. It just asks if you'll show up." Ms. Reaves smiled softly.

Desiree nodded, blinking away the sting behind her eyes.

"I'm trying."

"That's all any of us do," the teacher said, walking away to greet another student.

*****

Later, Desiree sat alone on the school steps, watching the sunset melt through the trees. The air smelled like rain waiting its turn.For the first time in a long time, she felt quiet – not numb, not high, not drowning. Just quiet.

Then her phone lit up.

Malik:

Hey stranger. Heard you home. Miss you.

Her fingers froze. The name looked the same, but everything around it had changed. She stared at the message until her eyes blurred. Her thumb hovered above the keyboard.

She typed I'm good. Then deleted it.

Typed Leave me alone, but deleted that too.

In the end, she locked the screen and set it face-down on the step. Sometimes silence is the loudest answer. She breathed deep, counted the exhale. The city lights blinked on, one by one – small promises in the dark.

That night, back home, she stood in front of the mirror again. Her reflection wasn't perfect, but it was honest. Mirrors never lie. The circles under her eyes were fading. The corners of her mouth remembered how to lift.

"New me," she whispered. This time it didn't sound like a lie.

CHAPTER SEVEN:
Relapse Season

Spring came early like it had somewhere else to be.

Sunlight slid under the blinds and warmed the carpet in strips. The air outside had that damp, green smell—cut grass, bus brakes, rain waiting its turn. Desiree woke before her alarm and didn't hate it. She ate toast and an egg without forcing it. She tied her curls up, tugged on jeans that fit on purpose, and stood in front of the mirror like a witness instead of a judge.

"You look like somebody," she told the girl in the glass. The girl didn't argue.

Group was at two. She got there ten minutes early because being on time kept the day from tilting. Ms. Lena nodded from the doorway like a lighthouse. Today's worksheet said Triggers & Plans in a font that tried too hard. Around the circle, people told the truth in chunks: payday, loneliness, mother's day, anniversaries of things you'd never post.

When it was her turn, Desiree cleared her throat. "I don't want to mess up and I also··· miss it." She let the words hang without prettying them up. "Both things are true."

"Thank you," Ms. Lena said, like Desiree had given her a gift instead of a confession. "Which one gets fed today?"

"Not the missing," Desiree said, almost smiling. "Not if I can help it."

She stayed busy after group because empty hours echo. She washed her pillowcases and hung them to dry so the sun could bless them. She sketched a window, then another, then the way light crawls across a wall. She texted Tati a meme and laughed out loud—not just the breathy Instagram "lol," the real kind.

At dusk, the quiet felt less friendly. Sirens stitched the evening together. The neighbors' TV leaked a game through the wall. Somewhere far, a bassline rolled like distant thunder. Desiree stood at her window and watched the street try to be good.

Her phone buzzed.

Unknown: You around? Heard you back. Clean work. On me.

She swallowed. The number wasn't saved but the voice behind those words wore familiar cologne. She set the phone face-down and slid it across the desk like it might bite.

Triggers and Plans.

Plan: breathe. Text Tati. Watch a dumb show with Ma. Sleep like it's medicine.

She made it through the night. One zero on the scoreboard that counted.

Relapse didn't come as a hurricane. It arrived as weather—gray and unconvincing, the kind that makes people skip umbrellas and get soaked anyway.

First it was a dream. Not one of the wild ones—just smoke curling in slow motion, a calm that felt earned. She woke with her tongue remembering a taste her mouth had no right to miss.

Then it was a bad day for no reason. A bus splashed her sneakers. A teacher made a joke that landed wrong. A cashier scanned every item like it had personally offended him. Tiny cuts, nothing fatal, but blood is blood.

Then Malik found the hole in her fence.

Malik: Proud of you. For real. You strong. Just checking in.

Malik: Can I see you? No pressure. Promise.

She typed no and deleted it because rejecting people felt like tempting fate. She typed maybe another time and deleted that too because it sounded like a coupon. In the end, she didn't answer. She silenced the thread. She put the phone under a book like weight could change intention.

It worked until it didn't.

*****

The station was warmer than outside, the air tasting like pennies and bleach. Desiree wasn't supposed to be there. She told herself it was just to ride two stops, clear her head, buy a churro from the lady with the foil pan. She told herself a lot of things that sounded logical if you muttered them fast enough.

Down on the platform, old heads ran small economies. Someone sold batteries. Someone sold advice. Someone sold sleep.

"Dez?" A voice slid out of a shadow.

She turned. Not Malik. Worse in a different way—one of his satellites with a grin that didn't reach his eyes.

"I'm good," she said before he could offer anything.

"Didn' t ask that," he lied, palm already opening. "Just checking. Heard you changed zip codes but the city still your cousin." He glanced at her shoes, at her hands, at the space where wanting lives. "Got a couple clean. Little white ones. Same as before, just better."

"I' m good." She meant it for two whole seconds, which is an eternity in a storm. Then the wind shifted. Her gums buzzed with memory. Her chest remembered floating.

"Just one," he said, like it was a reasonable portion of fire. "On the house."

Free is the most expensive price. She stared at the pill on his palm. The stamp was new. The shape was the same lie. Desiree thought about Ms. Lena' s circle. Thought about Tati' s laugh. Thought about her mother' s hands, cracked from sanitizer and grace. Her fingers moved before the rest of her could vote.

"Just one," she said, and hated how easy she sounded. She dry-swallowed and tucked the second pill into a pocket like a bad secret. The world didn' t change right away. She hated that, too.

She walked into the bathroom to wash her face and tell herself she had it under control. The mirror over the sink was cracked in three polite places. The light flickered like it couldn' t make up its mind.

Halfway through a sentence—you' re fine, you' re—her jaw softened, knees thought about quitting, vision pulled away from its body. The high rose too fast, like an elevator with broken brakes.

Uh-oh. Too strong. Too much. Too—

The floor translated what her mouth couldn' t. She could taste the cold tile. A far-off speaker announcing a delay like it mattered. The door opened and closed and opened again.

Somebody said "hey." Somebody else said "nah." Then a third voice, rough and kind at once: "Damn. Call 911. Now."

The janitor had seen this movie too many times to cry at the ending. Little kids flipping like fish out of water. He checked her breath, cursed softly, tilted her head. The world around Desiree turned to static, then a tunnel, then a pinhole of light, then−

Nothing. Desiree was gone...

*****

It's not dramatic, the way life leaves. It's bureaucratic. Paperwork. Pauses. A list of functions that clock out early. When consciousness slammed back into her, it was ugly. Air ripped into her lungs like a break-in. Her chest lurched. Everything hurt and meant she could still feel. People in blue hovered. Someone said her name wrong, then right.

"Desiree, can you hear me?" a voice called from a million miles away.

"Narcan given intranasal. Two." another voice said from the same area code.

"Respirations improving." the first said drawing closer. "Let's move."

"Stay with me, sweetheart." the second voice said as she arrived. The ceiling tiles flowed above her on a conveyor belt of fluorescent judgment. A paramedic with tired eyes squeezed her hand like a metronome. "Stay with me, sweetheart."

She wanted to tell him she hadn't gone anywhere, but her mouth didn't work. Sirens wrote a red line through the city. Somebody on a corner filmed for a story no one would finish. Traffic parted and closed again like a wound.

*****

The ER smelled like lemons and electricity. Curtains, beeps, whispers. Desiree blinked through it, nausea sitting in her throat like a secret. The clock on the wall pretended time was linear. Nurses moved like they'd practiced this choreography a thousand times.

Then her mother's face broke through the curtain like daylight through a boarded window. Evelyn's eyes were red but holding. Her shoulders squared like a protest sign. She didn't run; she arrived.

"Ma?" Desiree croaked. The word hurt and helped. Evelyn took her hand and squeezed until both of them knew the other was real.

"You almost died," she said, voice steady enough to build on.

"I didn't mean to," Desiree whispered. Shame tasted just like the station bathroom.

"They never mean to," Evelyn said, and kissed her forehead like a benediction. "I'm not losing you. Not to this. Not now."

The doctor said things about fentanyl and contamination and community resources. The social worker said "aftercare" and "beds available." Ms. Lena texted back within minutes: I'm on my way if they'll let me in. Everyone had words; only one thing mattered.

"Thirty days," Evelyn said, answering a question Desiree hadn't asked out loud. "Inpatient. No phone the first week. Then we see."

"Okay," Desiree said, because sometimes surrender is survival. The word didn't taste like defeat. It tasted like air. Still better than the bathroom floor. Her mother cried then, not messy—just the kind that waters something that might live. She scheduled an ugly cry for later because this wasn't the time, nor place. She gathered herself, smoothed the hospital blanket like you can tuck a person back into the world.

"We'll find you again," she said. "Both of us."

*****

She had bad dreams the first night and none the second. By day three her bones stopped buzzing. By day five her skin fit again. They made her drink water like it could wash the past out molecule by molecule. They made her write things down so she couldn't pretend later that she hadn't known.

A girl named Aaliyah had a laugh that belonged to a better planet and track marks that mapped this one perfectly. Seventeen, same as Desiree, eyes bright with defiance and grief. The first time they spoke was over a vending machine that ate a dollar.

"You remind me of my little sister," Aaliyah said, punching the glass gently.

"I don't even remind me of me," Desiree said, and surprised herself by smiling.

"We gonna fix that," Aaliyah promised. "Accountability partners. No punking out."

"I ain't no punk." Desiree was sure of.

"Bet." the girl nodded. They shook on it like kids making a blood oath without the blood. Later that night, back in the room with the plastic mattress and the buzzing light, Desiree wrote a four-line poem on the back of a schedule:

I was drowning in air,

calling out without sound.

Now I see the surface,

and I want to be found.

She pinned it to the corkboard above the desk and stared until the words felt like a map.

*****

Two weeks in, Ms. Lena made a visiting day and walked Desiree out to a bench beneath a crabapple tree that tried its best.

"You look more here," she said, nodding at Desiree's face, not the facility.

"I feel more here," Desiree said, touching her chest. "Still scared."

"Smart to be," Ms. Lena replied. "Fear ain't the enemy if it keeps you from the edge."

They sat quiet long enough to hear the insects auditioning for evening. Ms. Lena finally stood, dusted her hands.

"You don't owe anybody a performance," she said. "Not even me. Just keep showing up honest."

"I can do honest," Desiree said. "Most days."

"Most days is a miracle," Ms. Lena said, and left her with that.

*****

On day twenty-nine, Desiree walked to the art room and found an empty wall begging for something. She drew with charcoal until her fingers turned gray: a mirror angled toward a window, each catching the other's light. Underneath she wrote, small as a secret: Borrowed time is still time. Use it well.

Discharge came with a binder and a speech and a hug she actually returned. Evelyn waited outside with a tote bag and a smile that had learned to be cautious and still be real.

"Ready?" her mother asked.

"No," Desiree said honestly, then nodded. "But yeah."

They rode in silence awhile, radio low, city pretending not to eavesdrop.

"Ma?" Desiree said at a red light that felt like a pause button on fate.

"Yeah?"

"I want to live."

"I know," Evelyn said, and reached across to squeeze her knee. "Me too."

Desiree looked out the window at a skyline that had tried to kill her and also held all the people she loved. She pictured Tati laughing, Ms. Lena's nod, Aaliyah's bright eyes, her own hands steady around a pencil.

Relapse season was a climate, not a day. But even climates have clear mornings. At home, she stood in front of the mirror. The porch light clicked on by habit though the sun was still up, as if the house knew they'd need it tonight and the next and the next.

"New me," she whispered again, not like a slogan this time. Like a plan.

The girl in the glass looked back steady.Outside, sirens went somewhere else. Inside, she chose the next breath. Then another. Then another. She chose life.

CHAPTER EIGHT:
Echoes

Morning sunlight reached the corner of Desiree's room like it was sneaking in on tiptoe. The air smelled like detergent and hope – two scents that used to cancel each other out. Now, they felt like a good omen.

Her sketchbook was open on the dresser, a charcoal hand half-drawn and waiting.

She liked leaving drawings unfinished. It meant she still had more time.

"Breakfast!" her mother called from the kitchen. The sound of plates clinking, coffee dripping, and a gospel station humming low filled the house. That was the new normal, rhythm instead of chaos.

Desiree pulled on her hoodie and joined her.

"Morning," Evelyn said without looking up, flipping pancakes like grace was a muscle she'd learned to flex again.

"Smells good," Desiree said.

"You smell like sleep," her mother teased, sliding a plate across the counter. "Eat before it gets cold. Job fair's today, right?"

"Yeah. Art therapy booth. Ms. Lena said they need volunteers."

"Keep stacking the good days, baby." Evelyn smiled, proud and cautious at the same time.

"I' m trying."

"You ain' t trying — you doing." her mother corrected.

They ate in quiet rhythm. Forks, syrup, small talk. Healing disguised as breakfast.

At the community center, the air buzzed with voices and flyers. Tables with cheap tablecloths and half-deflated balloons lined the walls. Desiree helped hang prints of artwork from recovery participants — shaky first attempts, raw color, fragile courage.

Each one looked like someone learning to breathe again.

"Girl, yours gonna stop traffic," Ms. Lena said, adjusting Desiree' s frame. "Resilience, right?"

"Yeah. Feels like forever ago." Desiree sighed and shook her head.

"That' s a good sign," Ms. Lena said. "Means you' re growing faster than your memories."

"That' s poetic." Desiree laughed softly.

"Therapists gotta earn our keep somehow."

She felt good — light, almost steady — until her phone buzzed.

Group chat:

Aaliyah 🐧 2:47 AM

gone

Just that. No punctuation. No explanation. The world tilted. Sound drained from the room. Desiree stepped outside before the tears could embarrass her. The sun hit her too bright; the sidewalk blurred.

She called one of the girls from the program. The answer came through sobs.

It was Fentanyl again. Same batch, same corner. No Narcan this time. The words hit her chest like a rewind button pressed too hard.

Aaliyah's laugh, the vending machine, the promise — No punking out. She'd meant it. They both had. Desiree leaned against the brick wall and let her body shake. Anger, guilt, grief — it all came like weather she couldn't control.

"She was clean," she whispered. "She was trying."

"Trying's not enough," someone said behind her — Ms. Lena, quiet as prayer.

Desiree turned, face wet, throat raw. "Then what is?"

"Choosing again," Ms. Lena said. "Choices. Every day. Sometimes every hour."

That night, Desiree sat at her desk under the dim lamp. The house was asleep. The world wasn't.

She opened the sketchbook to a blank page. Her hands moved before her brain caught up — charcoal lines forming a portrait that wasn't quite Aaliyah but wasn't anyone else either.

She shaded the eyes last — wide, fierce, alive. Then wrote

under it:

"We don' t disappear. We echo."

The tears that fell weren' t for guilt this time. They were for remembrance.

Weeks passed. The ache softened but didn' t vanish. She visited schools with Ms. Lena to speak about substance awareness. The first time, her voice trembled; the second time, it didn' t. She saw herself reflected in too many young faces — curious, restless, one bad decision away from a story like hers.

"Don' t let pain be your teacher," she told them. "Listen before it shouts."

Afterward, a girl maybe fourteen lingered behind, head down. "My brother uses," she said. "Sometimes I think he' s already gone."

Desiree handed her one of her sketches — a mirror facing a window. "Keep this," she said. "You can still be his light."

The girl smiled like hope had just been loaned to her.

Back home, Desiree hung Aaliyah' s portrait above her desk. Next to it, she pinned her old "Resilience" drawing. Two girls, two fates, one reminder.

She whispered, "I' m still here," not as survival but as purpose.

And for the first time, the echo answered back — quiet, steady, alive.

It continues Desiree' s journey from survivor to voice — holding her scars up to the light, reconnecting with her purpose, and facing the ghost of Malik for the final time.

Same cinematic flow, same grounded tone — more maturity, but still Desiree's voice.

CHAPTER NINE:
Ripple Effect

The auditorium smelled like floor polish and nerves. Folding chairs squeaked as students shuffled in, whispering about who was supposed to be "the speaker." Desiree adjusted the mic three times before realizing it wasn't the mic she was scared of — it was the silence that came before speaking.

"Whenever you ready," the counselor said, stepping back with the kind of smile that meant don't run.

Desiree cleared her throat. Her palms were damp; her voice wasn't steady. But her heartbeat was honest.

"My name's Desiree Carter," she began. "I used to think I was invincible."

A ripple went through the crowd — small, curious, the sound of young people recognizing a familiar lie.

"I thought bad things only happened to other people. People on the news. People who didn't know better."

She paused. "Turns out, bad things don't need directions. They find you anyway."

A few kids nodded. One girl in the second row wiped her eyes. Desiree kept going.

"I took one pill. Then two. Then I stopped counting. I told myself I had it under control. Until I didn't."

She looked up at the faces staring back — some skeptical, some scared, some pretending not to care. "I died. They brought me back. Not everybody gets that second chance."

The words hung heavy but not hopeless. She let them breathe.

"I used to think recovery meant being perfect," she said softly. "Now I know it just means choosing better every day — even when nobody's watching."

The counselor clapped first. Then the room followed. The sound didn't feel like applause; it felt like permission. When she stepped off the stage, her knees were shaking, but her chest was light. She'd told her truth out loud, and the world hadn't ended.

"You have a gift, sweetheart," said a teacher with tired eyes and too many bracelets touched her arm. "That kind of honesty saves lives."

"Trying to save mine," Desiree smiled shyly. "I'm just trying to tell mine right."

*****

By the time she got home, the sky had flipped to pink and silver. The porch light blinked on by habit. Evelyn was trimming roses out front, dirt under her nails and peace in her face.

"How'd it go?" her mother asked, cutting another stem.

"I didn't pass out."

"That's a win." Evelyn laughed.

"They listened, Ma. Like really listened." Desiree laughed, leaned against the railing.

Evelyn looked up. "Good. Maybe somebody needed to."

They sat in the fading light, saying little. The hum of crickets filled the spaces where words didn' t need to live.

"Sometimes I still get scared." Desiree said after a while.

"Of what?" Evelyn reeled.

"Falling back. Losing myself again." she admitted.

Evelyn snipped another rose and handed it to her. "Then hold tighter next time."

Desiree pressed the stem between her fingers, careful of the thorns. "It still hurts."

"Good!" her mother proclaimed. Means you're still here."

*****

Saturday morning came slow. Desiree was halfway through a sketch – a ripple spreading from a single drop – when her phone buzzed with an unfamiliar number.

Unknown:

Heard you doing talks now. That' s cool. I been trying to get clean too.

Her stomach dropped. Malik. She stared at the screen like it might rewrite itself.

'Don ' t do it,' her brain said. Just one reply, her heart lied.

Desiree:

Proud of you. Stay focused.

He sent back a thumbs-up emoji and nothing else. It should've been closure. Instead, it was a ghost in daylight. She turned the phone off and went for a walk.

*****

The park was alive — kids shouting, joggers huffing, a street preacher blessing anyone within earshot. Desiree found an empty bench near the fountain and let the rhythm of the water fill her head.

That's when she saw him. Malik, or what was left of him. He was thinner now. Hoodie too big, eyes too old. He wasn't swaggering — just sitting near the edge of the basketball court, staring at the ground like the world had taken the shine out of him.

Their eyes met and emotions flickered like a old movie. Recognition. Surprise. Guilt. He stood up slowly. She didn't move.

"I'm not gonna start nothing," he said, hands raised. "I just—damn, Dez. You look··· good."

"So do you," she lied, because kindness doesn't always mean truth. They stood there a moment, suspended between past and present.

"I'm trying to get right," he said, voice shaking a little. "For real this time."

"I hope you do," she said. "But I can't walk that road with you."

"Yeah. I figured. You always had more light." He nodded like he'd already known.

"Maybe," she said. "But we both got shadows."

"Shadows..." Malik smiled, small and tired. "Guess that's true."

He turned to leave. She wanted to stop him, to say something that would undo what couldn't be undone. But she didn't. Some goodbyes don't need words. The sound of his footsteps faded. The fountain kept flowing.

That night, Desiree added to her sketch — more ripples, expanding outward, touching the edges of the page. In the center, she drew a single drop, falling but never lost.She thought about Aaliyah. About Malik. About her mother. About herself.

"Everything touches something," she whispered.

*****

Two weeks later, Ms. Lena called.

"There's an opening at the center — peer counselor for youth outreach. You interested?" she dared as if she didn't know the answer. Desiree froze.

"Me?" she reeled like people do when dreams manifest. Her addiction had become a nightmare. Helping people heal had become her dream.

"Yes, you. Who better?" Ms Lena laughed.

"When do I start?" she asked.

*****

On her first day, she stood in front of a new group — kids her age, younger, older. She didn't start with a speech. She started with a question.

"What' s the loudest thing you ever heard in your own head?" she wondered. They stared. Then, one by one, they answered.

The words poured out – fear, guilt, anger, hope. The room filled with stories. And in every voice, she heard an echo of her own. They weren't just like her, they were her. Talking to them was like talking to herself.

*****

That night, she stood before the mirror again.

The reflection staring back wasn' t the girl from the party, or the hospital, or the halfway house.

It was someone new – shaped by every mistake, every survival, every second chance. The light from her lamp bounced off the glass and scattered onto the walls like tiny constellations.

"I' m still here," she said. "And I' m not done yet."

The girl in the mirror smiled back, steady and sure. Outside, the city breathed. Inside, Desiree did too.

CHAPTER TEN:
Choices

The morning didn' t announce itself; it arrived.

Soft light slid across Desiree' s wall and stopped at the sketch of two mirrors facing a window. One caught the sun, the other returned it. Between them, her room felt like a small chapel.

She lay still and listened for trouble out in the world—sirens, shouting, the clatter of a city waking wild. All she heard was a pigeon on the ledge and a bus sighing down the block. Peace can be loud if you' re not used to it. Her phone buzzed.

Tati ♡: You up? Big day, counselor.

Desiree: Up. Don' t make me cry this early.

Tati ♡: No promises. See you at the center at 3. I' m bringing Snickers.

Desiree: Now I' m crying.

She grinned at the ceiling and swung her legs over the bed. A pair of clean jeans waited on the chair; a denim jacket hung from the doorknob. She tied her curls up and let two tendrils fall at her temples—an old habit that somehow felt new again.

In the kitchen, her mother was already in motion: kettle on, pan warming, gospel barely audible from the radio like a heartbeat under the morning. Evelyn looked up and smiled the smile she saved for good news and regular days.

"Egg?" she asked.

"Please." Desiree poured tea and watched the steam rise. "Today feels big."

"They all big," Evelyn said, sliding a plate across. "We just notice some more than others."

They ate in the kind of quiet that doesn' t need fixing. Halfway through her toast, Desiree cleared her throat.

"Ma?"

"Mm?" Evelyn hummed.

"I' m sorry." She let the word land without padding. "For the lies. For the nights. For stealing. For scaring you."

"I was scared," Evelyn said, eyes bright but steady. "But I was never leaving."

"I know." Desiree blinked fast. "Thank you for being the person I wanted to live for when I forgot how."

Evelyn reached across and squeezed her hand. "That' s what we doing now. Living."

They finished breakfast like a prayer you say with your hands.

*****

At the community center, the lobby smelled like lemon cleaner and crayons. A banner hung crooked from the far wall: ART + HEALING: YOUTH SHOWCASE & TALKBACK. Folding chairs lined the room; easels made a small forest. Desiree' s framed piece—Resilience—sat beside a brand-new

72

drawing: a ripple expanding from a single drop.

"That title?" Ms. Lena asked, tapping the frame.

"Consequences," Desiree said. "Not just the bad kind. Like··· what happens when something good keeps going."

"Appropriate," Ms. Lena smiled. She stepped back and lowered her voice. "By the way—board approved your hours to count toward a peer support certificate. You keep showing up like this, we'll get you paid to be who you already are."

"For real?" Desiree's mouth fell open.

"For real-for real," Ms. Lena said. "We don't waste miracles around here."

Before Desiree could float away, the door opened and a small crowd filtered in—parents, teachers, a handful of kids, and Tati carrying contraband candy like a bouquet. They hugged near the coat rack, laughing too loud, knocking an umbrella over on accident because friendship is clumsy when it's happy.

"You ready?" Tati asked.

"No," Desiree said honestly, then smiled. "But yeah."

*****

They started with art. A ninth-grader explained how a painting of a red door helped her name a memory; a senior read a poem that made two fathers in the second row wipe their eyes like dust had attacked them. When it was Desiree's turn, she didn't climb a stage; she stood between her drawings.

"I used to think choices were big and dramatic," she said, voice steady enough to sit on. "Like movies. But most of mine

73

were small. I said yes when I meant maybe. I said maybe when I meant no. I said 'I'm fine' when I wasn't."

A murmur of recognition moved through the room.

"One pill turned into two because I didn't want to feel regular. Then I didn't want to feel anything at all. I almost left this world without saying goodbye."

She took a breath and let it show on her face.

"Today, my choices are small on purpose. Water. Breakfast. Answer Tati's text. Tell my mom the truth. Draw instead of disappear. Help somebody else name their storm."

Silence, then hands, then the soft thrum of approval that feels like a room choosing you back.

A boy near the aisle raised his hand. "What do you do when you want it?"

"I tell on myself," she said. "To somebody safe. Then I do one next right thing. Not ten. One."

"What if you mess up?" a girl asked.

"I keep the appointment. I forgive the hour. I start again." She glanced at Ms. Lena, who nodded like a metronome. "You don't lose your right to choose because you chose wrong one day."

The boy lowered his hand. The room exhaled.

*****

Afterward, Desiree helped stack chairs while the crowd

thinned. A woman with a nurse's badge hugged Evelyn long and grateful. A teacher told Desiree she was a better speaker than most adults he knew. Ms. Lena fended off two donors with a smile sharp enough to sign checks.

Desiree stepped into the hallway for air and found the building's quiet. Her phone buzzed in her pocket.

Unknown: I'm checking in. Don't trip. I'm at intake now.

Her breath caught. Malik. She stared at the words until they blurred, then typed slow.

Desiree: I'm glad you're choosing. Keep choosing. One hour at a time.

Three dots appeared. Disappeared. Appeared again.

Malik: You saved me when you told your story. Just truth. Be safe, Dez.

She locked the phone and leaned her head against the cool cinderblock. Relief came mixed with sadness like rain with sun in it. Some goodbyes aren't doors. They're windows you finally stop climbing through.

"Everything okay?" Tati asked, poking her head out.

"Yeah," Desiree said, meaning it. "Let's get back in there."

*****

Evening brought a vigil two blocks away—a small crowd on the church steps holding candles for Aaliyah and three other young names the neighborhood had learned to pronounce too late.

Desiree hadn't planned to go—grief and microphones make a messy pair—but her feet led her anyway.

Someone handed her a candle. Wind threatened its small fire; she cupped her hand and watched the flame steady. The pastor spoke, then a grandmother, then a city councilman who meant well and said too much.

A woman from group nudged Desiree. "You want to say a word?"

She shook her head, then realized the word she actually meant was yes. She stepped up without notes and stood where everyone could see nobody special.

"I don't have a speech," she said. "Just a promise."

Heads lifted and all eyes were on her.

"I promise to say their names without making them smaller than the worst day of their life. I promise to keep Narcan in my bag and hope I never use it. I promise to text back. To knock. To insist. To keep choosing until choosing is a reflex."

Her candle burned close to her knuckles. She didn't flinch.

"I promise to love the people still here loud enough that the ones we lost hear it too."

She stepped back into the crowd. Someone hummed a hymn from deep in their chest. The block softened a little around the edges.

*****

Back home, the living room felt like a harbor. Evelyn set tea on the table and kicked off her shoes with a sigh that ended in a smile.

"You were good today," she said.

"I didn' t pass out," Desiree said again.

"That' s a good start but, not the only measurement." her mother chuckled.

They laughed and sank into the couch—mother and daughter who' d crossed a river and could finally see each other on the same bank. On the TV, a sitcom talked nonsense. Outside, a car door slammed. Somewhere far, fireworks pretended to be gunshots or the other way around.

"Ma," Desiree said quietly, "I think I want to finish the portfolio and apply to the arts magnet for senior year. Or⋯ start a small group at the center for girls. Maybe both."

Evelyn' s eyes glistened. "You don' t have to be just one strong thing. Be all of them."

"I' m scared of wanting," Desiree admitted.

"Want anyway," her mother said. "Then work."

＊＊＊＊＊

Near midnight, alone in her room, Desiree opened the sketchbook to a blank page. She wrote the word Choices at the top and let her hand move. Charcoal bloomed into a city skyline, a bridge, a girl at the halfway point looking both directions. Above her, a small constellation—five points of light—like friends, like promises, like exits.

At the bottom, she printed small—Borrowed time is still time. Use it well. She signed her name like a contract. The mirror across the room cleared her throat. Desiree faced it without flinching. The girl looking back was not a miracle or a warning. She was a person with a pulse and a plan.

"Okay," Desiree told her. "Here's what we're choosing tonight."

She held up a hand and counted on her fingers:

"One—water." She drank.

"Two—sleep." She turned the covers down.

"Three—tomorrow." She set an alarm with a name: Art + Group + Breathe.

"Four—honesty." She texted Ms. Lena: I want the peer cert. Tell me the hard parts.

"Five—joy." She pressed play on a song that made her twelve again for three minutes.

Outside, a siren headed somewhere that wasn't her. Inside, a quiet settled that didn't need help staying.

She slid into bed and let the city hum be the lullaby it had always refused to be. The room's last light came from her drawings—mirror catching window catching mirror—an infinite loop of returning brightness.

Before sleep took her, she whispered into the dark, the way people do when they've learned who's listening.

"I choose you," she told the part of herself that had waited through storms. "And I'll keep choosing."

The dark didn't answer but it never does. It didn't have to.

Morning would.

Author's Note:
A Real Choice

Desiree's story is fiction.

But what she went through is not.

Every day in America, more than 290 families lose someone to a drug overdose.

In 2023 alone, over 105,000 people died – and nearly 80,000 of them involved opioids, mostly fentanyl. Many of those who died weren't long-time users. They were first-timers, or people who thought they were taking something else. One pill. One hit. One moment that couldn't be undone.

Fentanyl is fifty times stronger than heroin and often hidden in pills that look safe.

There's no way to see it, smell it, or taste it – until it's too late.

If you or someone you love is struggling with addiction, please know this:

Help exists. Recovery is real. You are not alone.

National Helpline (SAMHSA): 1-800-662-HELP (4357)

Free, confidential support – 24 hours a day, every day.

Or visit findtreatment.gov for local options.

We can't rewrite the past, but we can choose the next page.

Every day we wake up is another chance to choose life, to reach out, to begin again.

Desiree's story ends with survival – let yours begin there.

ALTERNATE OUTCOME....

CHOICES

Candy Land

written and directed by

SA'ID SALAAM

"They ask you about intoxicants and gambling. Say, 'In them is great sin and [yet, some] benefit for people. But their sin is greater than their benefit."

Qur'an(2:219):

Dedicated to the scores of Americans who die from drugs everyday...

CHAPTER ONE:
New Year, New Me?

Desiree Carter stood at the bathroom mirror, her toothbrush hanging limply from her lips, her eyes locked on the reflection staring back at her. Deep brown skin, wide-set eyes, and thick curls piled into a lazy bun. The tiny gold studs in her ears glinted under the buzzing fluorescent light. She looked··· regular. Not ugly. Not pretty. Just regular.

"Junior year," she muttered through a mouthful of toothpaste. "Let's get it."

"Desiree, time! Bus gonna leave you!" her mom's voice rang out like clockwork from outside the bathroom door. She gave a slight tap with her dainty knuckles to put some pep in her step. She was once a cute teen and knew full well how cute teens get trapped in the mirror.

"Coming!" Desiree shouted. She spat, rinsed, and wiped her mouth with a towel before prying herself from the pretty girl in the mirror. She twirled through her bedroom grabbing her denim jacket and stuffing a Pop-Tart in her bag. The house smelled like coffee and cocoa butter, and the hallway carpet muffled her steps as she rushed down the stairs.

Her mother stood in the kitchen, hair tied back, work badge clipped to her polo shirt. Mrs. Evelyn Carter was a nurse—double shifts, no days off, and never late. No nonsense because life only allows so much nonsense before it rolls over you. She refused to be run over.

"You got everything?" she asked without turning around.

"Yeah." she quipped like teen girls will at that age. Minus the malice some of her friends harbored towards their mothers.

"Lunch?" Evelyn dared.   "And a Pop-Tart is not breakfast."

"Got it." Desiree snickered.

"You got your mind right?" her mother wanted to know. So many in their city did not and ended up in the same hospital she worked in.

Desiree smiled faintly. That was her mom's version of a pep talk. Her friend's mother didn't have them. Except for getting fussed and cussed out for one infraction or another. Unlike her friends she appreciated the love in the form of concern.

"I'm good, Ma." she assured and paused to look in the eyes they shared. The hazel orbs had flecks of green that made it impossible to look in and lie.

"Don't let nobody pull you off your path. Remember who you are." Evelyn demanded and showed the spirit that made her excel at work.

"I won't," Desiree vowed and gave a tight nod and leaned in for a kiss on the cheek. She didn't always know exactly who she was, but it felt good knowing someone believed she could be someone.

*****

The bus was already at the stop when she got outside, and she jogged the last few steps, waving at the driver. Inside, the usual chaos buzzed—fresh fits, new gossip, music blasting through AirPods. She slid into an empty seat and pulled her hood up. She was friendly and had friends, even if she occasionally ducked them. The gap between them and her mother took a second to cross.

85

Junior year was supposed to be her year. She'd made it through the awkwardness of freshman year and the fake-friends of sophomore season. This year, she had goals: all As, submit her art portfolio, maybe even apply for early college credit if she kept her GPA high. Her mom had already told her—there was no college fund. She wasn't mad. Just motivated.

"You want it, you gotta work for it." she repeated like her mother always told her. Meanwhile her friends were gossiping loudly and cackling even louder.

The bus lurched forward, and Desiree opened her phone. The school group chat was already going off. She scrolled through messages.

Tati: Y' all seen Malik's haircut??

Bree🔥: Man he got the summer fade but it's FALL lmaoo

🐸Jade: Issa new year. New rules. New bodies.

🔥Malik🔥: Y' all obsessed lol

🐸Jade: Desiree where u at? Slide thru lunch table 6

Desiree raised an eyebrow. Jade didn't usually talk to her directly. They weren't enemies or anything, just... different lanes. Jade was the type to cut class and post thirst traps in the bathroom mirror. Desiree was more 'honor roll, keep it lowkey.'

Because there was something flattering about being seen, and even worse to be bragged about.

*****

By third period, the buzz of a new year was wearing off. Teachers were laying down the rules—same speeches, different rooms. Desiree tried to focus, but her thoughts drifted. She kept thinking about that message. About table 6. What if she really did change things up this year?

At lunch, she usually sat with Tati and Cam, her best friends since middle school. They were good girls—goofy, safe, and predictable. But today, something tugged at her feet as she passed their usual spot. It would be kinda cool be cool.

"Desiree!" Cam called as Desiree walked by.

"Be right back," she said, already walking away.

Table 6 was louder, edgier, and smelled faintly like weed and lip gloss. Jade sat with her legs stretched across two chairs, nails like daggers and lashes batting like wings. Malik sat next to her, leaning back, arms covered in new tattoos. There was a spot open. Right next to them. Desiree stood awkwardly until Jade looked up.

"You made it girl," she smirked. "Sit down. We were just talking about the party this weekend."

"I don't really—" Desiree began to beg off.

"Girl. Don't say you don't party." Jade demanded like she was the boss of her just like she was the boss of the rest of the girls at the table.

"I mean, I, my moms..." Desiree stammered through a few possible excuses. Then settled on a, "Ok."

"See you then!" Jade insisted and turned away to the next pressing matter. "Girl y'all seen Malik hair cut..."

Desiree wasn't one of the cool kids but the way they all looked at her made her wonder. Maybe this year, she could be different. Maybe this year she could be cool.

*****

That night, Desiree laid in bed staring at the ceiling. The air was humid, and the fan above her clicked with every slow rotation. Her phone buzzed.

Bree🥚: You coming to Malik' s? Friday. Don' t be lame.

🎏Jade: Bring a chill fit. And an open mind.

Desiree didn' t respond. She just stared at the screen, feeling something unfamiliar in her chest. It wasn' t excitement but it wasn' t quite fear either. Her brows furrowed deeply until she figured out what it was. It was··· curiosity. And sometimes, curiosity is the first step off a cliff. After all, curiosity has killed many cats over the years.

CHAPTER TWO:
Just One Hit

Friday came too fast.

"I'm not ready!" Desiree announced as she stood in front of her closet, biting her thumbnail, trying to figure out what "a chill fit" even meant.

She didn't want to look like she was trying too hard, but she also didn't want to look like she didn't belong. After twenty minutes of changing, re-changing, and throwing outfits on the bed, she settled on ripped jeans, a cropped hoodie, and her newest sneakers. She brushed her curls into a high puff and added a little lip gloss. Not too much. Just enough.

"You ready," she told the cute girl in the mirror. Even flashed a smile, pout and blew a kiss. Then giggled like the kid she was.

She was ready to go until her phone buzzed again.

Tati ♡: You still coming over? Movie night!

Desiree's thumb hovered over the keyboard. She almost typed Can't tonight. Rain check? but stopped. Something about lying to Tati made her chest ache. No, she wouldn't lie. Instead, she just ignored it.

Old friends don't always adjust well to taking new friends. Which was why the girls at Jade's table all looked her up and down. They had all been 'selected' by Jade when she deemed them pretty enough, or cool enough to keep court with her.

*****

'I'm headed out,' Desiree texted her busy mother and got a 'thumb' in reply. They often talked through text even in the house if Evelyn had her door closed.

She told her mom it was a school project at Jade's house. She didn't even have to work hard at the lie—her mom was dead tired, halfway asleep in her scrubs before Desiree even grabbed her backpack and slipped out the door.

Malik lived on the west side, in an apartment complex known for loud music and louder arguments. Desiree had never been over there, but Jade promised someone would come get her. Sure enough, a black car pulled up at the corner near her street. Inside were Jade, Bree, and a guy she'd never met—tall, with golds in his mouth and arms draped casually over the steering wheel like he owned the city.

"That's Dez?" the guy asked.

"Yeah, she cool," Jade replied, motioning her in. "Hop in."

"Bet!" Desiree cheered and hopped into the back seat. She felt cooler already having heard him use her nickname.

Desiree's stomach fluttered. She climbed in, trying to act normal. Bree handed her a drink in a plastic cup. It smelled fruity and sweet, like something you'd sip at the beach. She took a cautious sip. It burned, but she didn't let it show. The sweet taste stuck to her lips so she gave a lick. At the exact moment the driver glanced in the rearview. He smiled and nodded as if the lick were for him.

"Welcome to the real world," Bree giggled, raising her own cup.

"The real world..." Desiree repeated and paused to think. Then lifted the cup for another sip.

*****

Malik's place was already packed. The music was loud enough to shake the walls, and the smell of weed hit her like a wave as soon as they walked in. People were dancing, laughing, play-fighting. Cups littered the counters, and someone had already knocked over a lamp in the living room.

Desiree pressed her back against the wall and looked around wide eyed. The people were loud and lively like they were having the times of their lives. Like this was success and they had made it. They looked happy which somehow confused her.

"Come here gurl...." Jade said led her to the kitchen and poured her another drink.

"Huh?" Desiree asked as if she had done something wrong.

"Loosen up," she said. "You acting like a narc."

"Narc?" Desiree reeled. She wasn't about that life but didn't want to be a narc either. So she lifted her cup and knocked her drink down to prove it.

"That's what's up!" Jade cheered and laughed.

Desiree laughed nervously, trying to let the music and energy carry her. But everything felt like it was moving too fast—too much bass, too many flashing lights, too many unfamiliar faces. She blinked as her cup was quickly filled again. This was a party so she leaned against the counter and took another sip.

*****

It was an hour later when she found herself sitting on the

back porch with Malik, a small group of kids passing a blunt between them. The air was cooler outside, and the music was muted by the sliding glass door. It felt calmer. Safer.

"You ever smoked?" Malik asked, holding the blunt between his fingers. He tilted his head like a dare and Desiree shook her head.

"I never used drugs before," she admitted.

"It ain' t that deep," he said. "It' s just weed. Better than stress. Better than school. Better than pretending."

"True! Word! I know that's right!" The others laughed and nodded like it was gospel. Malik took a hit and passed it her way. She hesitated.

"Just one hit," he said. "That' s it."

"Hit, hit, hit, hit..." her peers pressured.

Desiree stared at the blunt like it held a decision bigger than her whole life. She thought about her mom' s voice, about Tati' s text, about her GPA, her dreams. Then she looked at Malik. At Jade. At everyone else smiling like life was easier on their side.

Her shoulders shrugged and she took it. Analyzed it, scrutinized it, then lifted to her lips and inhaled.

The burn hit her throat first, sharp and dry. She coughed hard, eyes watering, while everyone laughed good-naturedly.

"Mmhm! That's that gas!" her new friends cheered.

"First-timer," someone said, handing her a bottle of juice. The light hearted laughter didn't feel like getting laughed at so she laughed too. Then basked in the instant glow creeping through her body. She felt dizzy but warm, giddy and giggly. Her body felt floaty, like she was wrapped in clouds. The colors around her got brighter, the music sweeter. The knot of anxiety in her chest untied itself slowly.

'This...' she thought, is what peace feels like.

For the first time in a long time, she didn't feel like she was trying so hard. She wasn't overthinking, over-planning, over-doing. She was just··· here. And it felt good.

By the time she got home, it was nearly 2 a.m.

The house was dark, her mom long asleep. Desiree tiptoed to her room and collapsed on the bed fully dressed. Her head spun slightly, but she was still smiling.

She scrolled through her phone, checking her socials. Jade had tagged her in a blurry selfie. Desiree looked happy. Pretty, even. The comments were full of flame emojis and "who dat?" questions.

She felt seen, she felt included. She felt cool, but most of all, high. Her smile widened but deep down, she wondered how long that feeling could last. She liked this feeling.

CHAPTER THREE:
Chasing Chill

The first time getting high took a lot. Pros, cons, pressure from peers and a smile from Malik. The second time wasn't even a question.

"Hmm," Jade hummed to hold the smoke in her lungs as she passed the weed.

"Thanks," Desiree said. Now she didn't hesitate when Jade passed her the blunt after school behind the bleachers.

The group had gotten tighter—Desiree was officially "in" now. People she barely knew before nodded when they passed her in the hallway. Her Instagram was buzzing. She wore lashes now. Bought new jeans that hugged her hips. Switched her bio to: vibes > validation.

Because she was definitely feeling the vibes. She liked the way it made her feel. Not just the weed—but the life.

"Gurl!" Desiree heard herself cheer. The old her heard the new her and smiled.

"Right!" Jade cheered along with her new right hand girl. Her other friends had to take a back seat to the new addition to the crew.

Desiree started skipping homework. Not all the time—just here and there. She was still pulling Bs. Her mom didn't notice yet. Still too tired from work to check the online portal or ask too many questions. Desiree made sure to keep things clean at home.

Dishes done. Bed made. Smile ready.

A perfect little cover for the life she was building outside those walls.

*****

By October, weed was a regular thing. After school, on the weekends, before parties, sometimes even before first period if she was really anxious. She kept a mini deodorant can in her bag and a travel-sized bottle of body spray to cover the scent. She'd gotten good at hiding her increasing weed habit.

But she wasn't good at everything and it was just a matter of time before it started to catch up with her. She failed her first test in Algebra II.

Mrs. Reaves handed it back face-down, but that didn't stop the red 57% from burning through the paper like it was tattooed on her skin. Desiree stared at it, her stomach twisting.

The woman had seen it enough to know what was happening. Seen it enough to know it was bigger than her.

"Dang..." Desiree reeled as she blinked to process her first failing grade.

"You okay?" Tati asked softly from the next seat. They hadn't really been talking like before. It was mostly weird smiles and quick nods in passing.

"Just a bad day." Desiree shrugged and covered the grade so her friend wouldn't see it.

"You been having a lot of those lately." her friend offered like a real friend would.

"I'm fine." Desiree declared and looked away. But her

95

real friend could clearly see she wasn't.

She couldn't focus the way she used to. Her thoughts jumped like skipping rocks. Her motivation dipped. Everything that used to matter started feeling small—grades, college apps, art contests. What even was the point?

Besides, everyone said junior year was hard. Maybe this was just normal.

*****

That Friday, at another party, she smoked again. And drank, but it wasn't the fruity stuff this time—it was clear and bitter and burned her throat like battery acid. Someone called it "white girl vodka." She didn't care. It worked.

Her mind blurred. Her shoulders dropped. She danced like nobody was watching—even though everybody was. She was the new meat everyone wanted to meet.

Malik found her in the kitchen, leaned back on the counter with a blunt in one hand and a red cup in the other. He smiled when he saw her.

"There she go," he said and flashed a smile.

"There he is," she repeated. Most of the new her was just repeating what the cool people said and did. Now she looked and sounded cool, just like them.

They talked. Laughed. He called her pretty. She blushed, or maybe it was the liquor. When he leaned in, she didn't stop him. Not when he kissed her. Not when his hand slid across her lower back. She didn't kiss him back but didn't stop him either. She just let it happen. She let everything happen.

The things Jade and the other girls talked about openly. They were women while she was a little girl. Until now. Now she was a woman too.

*****

"Ugh!" Desiree groaned next morning when she woke up in Jade's guest room. Her head was pounding. Her mouth tasted like ash. Her clothes were wrinkled and she wasn't even sure if she still had her earrings. She checked her phone.

7:12 AM

12 missed calls: MOM

3 texts: TATI 'You good?. You ain't answer none of my calls. Whatever. Just don't forget who really care about you.'

"Ugh!" she moaned again put the phone down and buried her face in the pillow. Guilt clawed at her chest, but she was too tired to cry. She would have cried too if she hadn't spotted the half blunt in the ashtray. Her brain reasoned why feel bad when she could feel could.

"Hmp!" she answered and lit the blunt up. The problems dissipated in the plume of smoke she blew towards the ceiling. Soon the guilt was replaced by a smile and acknowledgement, "I'm a woman now."

*****

"That's what we doing now?" Evelyn asked when her daughter traipsed in the next afternoon. Spending the night out was bad enough so she hung out most of the morning.

"Stayed over at Jade's," she shrugged to minimize the situation.

"And that's that huh?" her mother laughed without a trace of

97

humor.

"Ma, I done spent a night out before," Desiree reminded.

"Yeah. Sleep overs with Tati and them. I don't even know this Jade," Evelyn fussed but caught herself. Fussing and fighting would make things worse, not better. And it definitely wouldn't stop the teen from doing what she wanted to do. "I just hope you know what you're doing."

"I'm just doing me ma," she shrugged again. The problem was even she wasn't sure exactly who she was.

"I see," the woman sighed. She noticed the changes over the last few months but she watched the girl change constantly from the day she brought her home from the hospital. It would be nice if babies stayed babies, but they don't. They grow up and you never know what you'll end up with.

Back at school the next week, her teachers started noticing. Her drawings were darker. Sloppier. Her essays came in late. If at all. She lost interest in the things she once found so interesting. This new life, pop life now had her full attention.

"You have so much talent," her English teacher said gently one afternoon, handing back a half-finished assignment. "What's going on, Desiree?"

"I don't know," she whispered. And she really didn't since the new her was moving the old her out of the picture. She could once spend all day shading and perfecting a picture but now she had no desire to draw. She did like to smoke with her new friends so much that she started smoking all by herself.

*****

"Hey you," Malik cheesed after school, she met up with him near the basketball courts. He told her he had something new. Something stronger.

"Hey yourself," she blushed and lowered her had at what had happened between them. He cracked that knowing smile and produced some candy. "What is that?"

"Edibles," he said, holding up a pack of colorful gummies. "Last longer than smoke. Hit smoother."

He extended his palm but Desiree hesitated. Even she realized how one thing seemed to lead right into another. From the sickly sweet drink to drinking clear liquor. From smoking once a weekend with friends to smoking every day, even by herself. One thing always led to another until she was led into a bedroom.

"You trust me, right?" Malik leaned in and asked. It was more like a dare since she trusted him with so much already. But she wasn't sure if she could trust anybody. Not even herself anymore.

"I guess," she sighed. Her head still nodded as she plucked one from his hand and popped one in her mouth. "What's it gonna do?"

"Make you feel like Silver Surfer riding on the clouds!" he cheered enthusiastically since that was how he felt at the moment.

That night, her world melted. The high was heavier—more like floating than flying. Everything slowed. She couldn't even feel her fingers. She laid on her bed, staring at the ceiling fan like it was a planet spinning above her.

"Whoa..." she reeled as she rode the clouds.

There was no noise, no pressure. No fear. Just chill. For once, Desiree didn't dream. And that was the scariest part—because even her dreams had went silent.

CHAPTER FOUR:
Bottom Shelf Dreams

"Tuh!" Desiree huffed at her reflection. Even she realized she looked different now so she just didn't look. She felt good and that was all that mattered.

Not because of anything obvious—her curls were still full, her skin still smooth, her eyes still wide. But something behind them had dimmed. Like a lightbulb running low on power. Probably because she hadn't drawn anything in two weeks. Artists have to paint, write or sculpt on a regular basis to feel regular.

Not because she didn't want to. She just··· couldn't. Every time she picked up a pencil, her hand would freeze. Her thoughts would scatter. Her brain felt slow and loud at the same time. Like too many radio stations overlapping in her head, none of them clear.

Art used to be her therapy. Now, even it felt like a chore.

"I know what..." Desiree comforted when she remembered the gummie in her purse. She scrambled to get it out and into her mouth. All that was left now was wait for it to kick in.

*****

Desiree's mom had noticed before she did. Only because she ignored the signs along with her reflection. The woman knew her daughter had to choose her own path and did her best to give her the best example to see. She bit her tongue until she couldn't anymore and had to speak up.

"You been off lately," Mrs. Carter said one evening, folding laundry on the couch while the news buzzed in the background. "Grades slipping. You stay in your room. You barely eat."

"I'm fine." Desiree replied but didn't look up from her phone.

"I know something's wrong, baby. I can feel it." Mrs. Carter sighed.

"That's the thing, I'm not a baby," Desiree clenched her jaw. "I'm fine. I just got a lot on my mind."

"Is it a boy?" she wondered since that's when most teen girls challenge their mothers.

"No, Ma." she sighed loudly and rolled her eyes. Her mind flashed to Malik but wasn't sure what to call that.

"You sure it ain't something else?" Her mother's voice dropped. "You using something?"

"What? No!" she vowed indignantly. Desiree's chest seized as if insulted by the question. She swallowed quickly, keeping her face still. "Why would you even ask that?"

"Because I ain't stupid." Evelyn reminded since she must have forgotten. "I'm a nurse you know! Plus, I was young once myself."

"I said I'm fine." Desiree insisted and stood up.

"Can't be fine talking to me like that!" Evelyn shot back and stood as well. The standoff lasted a whole second before Desiree sank back down to the sofa.

"My bad ma," she tapped out and leaned back.

"I'm just saying slow down. Don't be in such a hurry to grow up. Ain't nothing in them streets. Nothing good," Evelyn assured. "I see kids who grew up too fast in the emergency room every night. Some become mothers too soon. Some become dead, too soon!"

"I'm good ma," Desiree pleaded and left the room before the tears could follow her.

*****

"Ho-hum," Desiree chimed when she saw Jade stunting for the Gram. She was riding around in a Scat Pack Charger with her latest boo thang. Desiree thought about calling Tati but had went so hard to prove she didn't need her to need her now.

She cracked her window open and fired up a blunt. She hung halfway out to make sure all of the smoke wafted above and not back into the house. She was content to get high alone until she got a text from Malik.

Slide thru. Just me and you.

On my way

She text back and was all the excuse she needed to get out of the house. She could have asked for permission but decided to leave without it. That way she didn't have to answer any questions. She knew full well why he invited her over and didn't want to lie to her mother.

Evelyn heard the front door open and close. It opened and closed every day but this was the first time she actually wondered if her child would make it home. She saw plenty every day who didn't. Meanwhile Desiree walked briskly a few blocks until she reached the once majestic brownstone. It had been chopped into small apartments like the one Malik rented.

His apartment was dark, lit only by the TV screen and a scented candle burning low on the table. It smelled like cinnamon and something chemical. Desiree sat close to him on the couch, her knees touching his.

"You good?" he asked, brushing a strand of hair from her face.

"Not really. Me and my moms. She been tripping lately," she sighed. She blamed her mother's reaction to her new lifestyle instead of the lifestyle itself.

"I got something for you..." he said and reached behind the couch. She hoped it was a gift, rose maybe but he pulled out a bottle—cheap liquor, half-full. No label.

"Here," he said. "It' ll help."

"What is it?" she asked but didn' t hesitate to take the cup when he poured.

"A lil sum," he replied and smiled. The smile was enough for her and she drank. One sip turned into two. Two turned into too many.

"Relax, you too tense." Malik said and now had a reason to massage her shoulders. A reason to touch her and she didn't resist.

*****

Desiree didn' t remember much of that night. Just flashes. The way the room spun. How the walls felt like they were closing in. She woke up alone in his bed. Her clothes mostly on, but her hoodie was backward and her phone was dead. She sat up slowly, the taste of last night still in her mouth.

"Malik?" she called towards the sounds coming from the front. She finished dressing and spun the hoodie around correctly before stepping out and finding Malik in the kitchen, shirtless, making eggs.

She didn't say anything. Neither did he. Nothing needed to be said since it was what it was. She did smile though since she liked what it was. They made some small talk over breakfast but Desiree kept reflecting back to her mother. She had a right to do her and live her life. She just hated disappointing the person who had once been her best friend. She traded her for Tati, then Jade. Malik smiled again and she was ready to make the next trade.

The walk home felt longer than it should've. Her feet were heavy. Her thoughts were heavier as she tried out excuses and explanations out loud as she walked. She didn't like none of them but preferred them to the truth.

She got home around 9 a.m. and slipped through the front door. Her mom was already gone, probably working another shift. Desiree collapsed on her bed without changing. Her eyes burned, but no tears came.

She wasn't even sure what she felt anymore. Shame? Fear? Anger? Or maybe nothing at all. She awoke a few hours later and followed the sounds into the kitchen where her mother was cooking. She braced herself and prepared to freestyle answers to whatever questions. Except none came. Her mother had already said what she had to say now it was up to her to follow or not.

*****

The next few weeks were a blur of drinking, smoking and spending nights at Malik's. It was unsustainable and something had to give. She had to cut back on something so she chose school. She started out showing up late until stopped showing up to first period altogether. Jade had a fake doctor's note plug. She would need the extra time when Malik started giving her little white pills.

"What's that?" she smiled as he placed one on his tongue and swallowed it down.

104

"Percs," he said and held one out for her. She extended her hand but he shook his head. She smiled mischievously and stuck out her tongue. "There you go..."

"What does it do?" Desiree asked in the wrong order since she had swallowed first.

"It's like weed but better," he promised.

"Oh ok!" she cheered since she really liked weed and this was supposed to be better.

He was right. They made her forget everything: school, her mom, her anxiety, the night she couldn't remember. The pills erased it all. For a while.

The first day it was one pill. Then one pill a day. Then two. And she started to change even more.

*****

"There go your girl!" Bree hissed when she spotted Desiree in school. She turned her nose up to signal she had given up on her after giving her shade. Tati had tried to talk to her once when she cornered her in the hallway between classes. She gave her shade as well but Tati still wouldn't give up on her.

"Dez, I don't know what's going on with you, but this ain't you." Tati snapped when she caught her at her locker. They had side by side lockers since grade school because they were once inseparable.

"You don't even know me anymore." Desiree snorted and snarled.

"I knew the you who stayed up drawing all night. The one who used to make me playlists and say school was your escape. I knew that girl. I don't know this girl." Tati shot back loud

105

enough to turn heads.   "I ain't seen that girl in months!"

"Then maybe stop looking for her." Desiree turned away. Her jaw was tight but she felt like she wanted to cry. Malik hadn't called in days which meant she was officially out of the free pills he provided her.

Asking her mother for money wasn't an option since she slacked on her chores so much Evelyn just did them herself. She certainly couldn't ask the woman for a few bucks to get high. There was only one thing to do so she stole twenty bucks from her mother's purse.

It was the first time. It wouldn't be the last. But she justified it by telling herself it was temporary. That she'd get clean later. That she just needed a break from life. That this was her phase—the kind everyone had.

But deep down, a small voice inside her whispered the truth: You're not in control anymore.

CHAPTER FIVE:
Mirrors

"This girl don't know how to return people's stuff..." Evelyn grunted as she searched her daughter's room. She wasn't one of those mothers who routinely searched their child's personal space but Desiree was one of those children who liked to use their mother's stuff without asking. It wasn't the not asking that bothered her most, it was the forgetting to return it.

Evelyn noticed the twenty dollar shortage in her purse but blamed everything but her daughter. Desiree had always been trustworthy and loyal, except when it came to phone chargers, lip gloss and hair brushes. She was looking for the charger this time but came up the lip gloss she forgot about.

"This is my favorite!" Evelyn growled and tucked it in her pocket. She was already irritated that Desiree had ignored three texts and come home after curfew again–when she saw a small plastic bag tucked behind the jewelry box.

At first, she thought it was candy. But her gut told her different. Plus she knew better, all the signs were there. She opened it, and the smell hit her immediately–bitter, chalky. Pills, light blue, stamped with a number.

"Ok. Ok..." Evelyn sighed. She didn' t scream, she didn' t cry. She just sat on the edge of the bed, her fingers trembling around the bag. She knew she had to do something but wasn't sure what. Ignoring the signs was no longer an option.

*****

"Pop a Xany and chill, got my face on the bills..." Desiree rapped as walked through the door twenty minutes later. Her hoodie smelled faintly of weed and her eyes were glassy. She barely made it past the living room when she saw her mother waiting for her. The look in her eyes made Desiree freeze. "Sup ma?"

"Sit down," Mrs. Carter said coldly. Desiree didn' t move and glanced towards the door like she might make a run for it. "I said sit. Down."

She dropped her backpack and sank into the couch with a deep sigh. Desiree knew the day would come when her crap caught up with her. Except, she was doing so much crap lately she wasn't sure which crap this was about. Until her mother stood, holding the plastic bag up like it was evidence in a courtroom.

"What is this?" Evelyn asked rhetorically. She was a whole registered nurse and knew good and well what they were. She even second guessed herself and ran the number on the pill to be sure. Now she was as sure about the missing twenty dollars from her purse.

"It' s not mine." Desiree blurted. It was the first thing that came to mind so she decided to ride with it. Her mother really wanted to believe it but wouldn't ignore the signs.

"You really think I' m stupid? You really gon' lie to my face?" Evelyn moaned. She was more hurt than angry but this was tilting the scale.

"It' s just–just something a friend gave me. It' s not even that serious." Desiree dismissed.

"Not that serious?" Her mother' s voice cracked. "You got drugs in my house, Desiree. Pills. Pills. You know how many kids are dying off this stuff?"

"I ain't one of them. Look, see. I'm right here..." she snapped, stood and spun around. "Alive!"

"You could be! One wrong pill, one time, and I'm burying you in the ground!" Evelyn pleaded. She saw it literally every day of her life. Some made it through just fine but came back second and third times. Some fried their brains beyond repair and became mental patients. The others died.

"Why you always act like I'm some criminal? You don't even see me anymore." Desiree asked, voice rising. Mrs. Carter stared at her daughter, eyes full of disbelief and heartbreak.

"You think I don't see you? Baby, I see everything. I see how tired you are. I see the bags under your eyes. I see your spirit disappearing. I see a little girl I barely recognize anymore." the woman moaned and shed a tear.

Desiree couldn't bear the tears so she looked away. That's how she got through her own conscious gnawing at her. How she got around Tati's advice and Bree's scorn. Just ignore it, don't acknowledge it.

"Go to your room," her mother said finally. "We'll talk in the morning."

"Ok," Desiree agreed but they didn't. Because that night, Desiree snuck out again. Malik wasn't answering so she went another direction.

*****

"Hey girl!" Jade greeted as she opened the door to her house. "Come on in."

"Y'all having a party?" Desiree wondered since the house was loud, dirty, crowded.

109

"No. Why you asked?" Jade wondered and looked around the everyday chaos she lived in.

The house belonged to her grandmother and was filled with cousins, aunts, uncles and strays. There was no food, just leftover fast food bags and half-smoked blunts on the counter. These were relatives, not family and everyone was on their own. But there were pills and that's all Desiree wanted.

"You got anything?" she asked when they reached the cluttered room Jade shared with an unknown and fluctuating number of girls from five to thirty-five. It smelled of pee and menthol but no one seemed to notice.

What Desiree noticed was the amount of clothes on the floor, on top of the dresser and shoved in the small closet. She wondered how the fly girl managed to stay fly in the midst of this mess.

"You know I do!" Jade cheered and did a little dance as she removed a bag of pills from her bra. It was the safest place in the house since everyone here stole. "You know Robbie broke me off!"

"Girl thanks!" Desiree grunted and greedily gobbled a pill. She dry swallowed since she didn't have time to find something to drink. She hated the antsy feeling that came from being sober so she just stayed high as much as possible. Which wasn't as possible as it once was when Malik was supplying it.

*****

"Enough is enough!" Evelyn decided when her daughter hadn't returned by Saturday. She understood she was embarrassed but she'd been gone for two days now.

Mrs. Carter called the school first but she hadn't been seen in days. She knew her friends so she called around to Tati and Bree who hadn't seen her in a week. Tati said she had been hanging with Jade's house. Nothing. No one had seen her.

110

She was about to file a missing persons report when Desiree came stumbling in at 2 a.m., reeking of smoke, eyes red, hoodie inside-out. She had partied herself out and needed to crash for a few days. Evelyn almost didn't recognize the stranger when she walked down.

"Aahh!" she gasped and nearly broke down. Then remembered that wasn't an option. "Get in the shower. Then pack your bags."

"What?" Desiree challenged. She needed some rest and wasn't in the mood for a lecture.

"You heard me. You need help. Real help. I already called a program." her mother stood firm. Trying to be a friend is what got them here. Now she was being a mother.

"I don't need rehab." Desiree vowed. "I just need some rest!"

"You don't get to decide that." her mother shot back.

"You think sending me away gonna fix this? You think that's love?" Desiree laughed bitterly.

"I think love is watching your child destroy herself and not letting it keep happening. You're not dying. Not on my watch!" Evelyn shouted.

Desiree never saw her mother like this and thought twice. The fire in the woman's eyes actually scared her. Scared her enough to comply. She took that shower and packed that bag. Next stop was a residential treatment center.

*****

They say the first night is always the hardest and Desiree proved them right. She screamed, shoved a chair and slammed the door to her room so hard a picture fell off the wall. Her shouts were absorbed in the padded walls designed to protect those who liked to punch walls.

Once she wore herself she stretched out on the bed but didn't sleep. She just stared at the ceiling, heart racing, brain fogged, feeling like a caged animal. Of course this her mother's fault. Then again Malik since he had a new girl. Then Jade's fault too since her house was too nasty and crowded to sleep. It was everyone's fault except her own.

Somewhere during the night she realized she didn't want this life anymore. Her head nodded in agreement but she didn't know how to stop. The lockdown facility gave her no choice since she couldn't get drugs no matter how much her skin crawled.

The next few weeks was a blur and she was released back home to her gracious mother. It wasn't quite over with since she was admitted into a short-term outpatient program. Three days a week, two hours a day. Group sessions. Boring videos. Fake counselors who didn't understand her. People twice her age talking about crack and meth and prison time.

'Tuh. These people are dang junkies!' Desiree thought to herself as people gave their testimonials.

There was the once upon a time suburban housewife who got hooked on pain pills. They helped with the pain but hurt when she kept on using them after the pain was gone. She spent the household budget until it became a problem. Then stole whatever her husband was careless enough to leave in his wallet or pockets. Then sold things out of the house until even the kids toys were gone. There was nothing else to sell except herself, so she sold that too.

'Tuh!' She huffed again because she didn't belong here. Or maybe she did. She was there after all.

*****

"You' re not broken, Desiree," one of the counselors, a middle-aged Black woman named Ms. Lena, said one day after group. "You' re just hurting. Hurt people make hurt choices."

She watched Desiree every time and agreed with her that she didn't belong her. She wasn't like the rest since she had polite mannerisms and it was easy to tell someone invested time and love into the girl. Desiree didn' t respond but Ms. Lena refused to give up.

"You ever look in the mirror and not recognize who' s looking back?" she cocked her head and dared.

"Every day." Desiree admitted and swallowed hard.

"That means the old you is still in there. She ain' t gone. Just hiding." Ms. Lena cheered at the breakthrough. She smiled broadly but Desiree blinked hard, trying not to cry.

"She' s scared," she whispered. "She don' t know what to do."

"Then we gon' help her figure it out." Ms. Lena nodded. She was determined not to let this one get away. The woman had been to too many funerals, she would not fail.

"Ok," Desiree squeaked out. She cleared her throat and spoke up for herself. "Yes! Ok!"

*****

That night, Desiree stood in front of her mirror. For the first time in a long time she took a good look at herself and didn't like what she saw. She had gotten so far away from who she was she barely recognized her own self.

Her eyes were sunken and sullen. Her lips dry and wrinkled.

Her hoodie sagged off her shoulders from the weight she lost chasing the next high.

But when she stared long enough, she could almost see the girl she used to be. The one who stayed up all night sketching, who cried during sad movies, who used to laugh so hard she couldn' t breathe.

She touched the glass and nearly smiled at the lost long friend.

"I miss you," she whispered.

But mirrors don' t talk back. They just reflect and always tell the truth. Mirrors don't exaggerate or lie, they only show you what you' ve become.

CHAPTER SIX:
Little White Pills

Desiree was off to a strong start but didn't last in the program. She started skipping group after the second week. Told her mom she was going but never showed up. Instead she hung around parking lots, trap houses, back seats of cars with tinted windows. Anywhere she could numb the ache inside her chest.

Fighting was too hard but the pills were easy. The pills were always waiting, readily available. It started with Percs. Then something stronger. People she barely knew handed her things with names she couldn't pronounce. Xanax. Oxy. Roxy. Sometimes, they said it was "just to sleep," or "just to vibe."

Not that it mattered. All that mattered was the feel. She stopped asking questions. Because what did it matter if she felt good?

"Doesn't everyone want to feel good?" she reasoned, and she was right.

But most people feel good by doing good. By doing for family and community. By serving God and mankind. Doing good is its own reward since it reciprocates by making the doer feel good about the good they do.

But Desiree was doing bad. Doing worse with each day, each pill, each missed class. The first time she stole from a stranger, it was at a house party. Someone left their purse on the counter while rolling a blunt in the kitchen. Desiree slipped the cash and a bottle of pills out before anyone noticed.

The second time, she took from her mom's dresser. Not money—just a pair of earrings. Pawned them for $40. She didn't even feel bad anymore. Just numb, nothing mattered.

If anything, it scared her how easy it had become. School became a distant memory. Because something had to give. Getting high and getting good grades didn't match so she stopped going. Desiree's name was called during roll call, but she hadn't been to class in weeks.

The whole crew was falling off since birds of a feather always flock together. Jade was suspended for fighting. Bree dropped out. A person is like their friends so Tati became a loner.

Malik was around sometimes, but distant. Using heavier now. Slurring his words. His apartment was quiet and empty, always cold. He stopped answering texts unless she had something to trade. Desiree realized she didn't love him anymore. She wasn't sure if she ever did.

*****

One night, Desiree found herself walking along the side of the highway, hoodie pulled tight, no idea how she got there. It was cold and her nose was bleeding slightly—dry air and too many chemicals. She sat under a bridge and stared up at the stars.

The present was a murky blur so she remembered being ten and thinking she was going to be an artist. She remembered painting sunflowers in fourth grade and getting a ribbon at the school art fair.

She remembered her mom crying when she won the middle school portfolio competition.

And now, here she was.

High as kite. Alone. Under a bridge. Her mother now cried,

116

hoping this wasn't the day one of those dead kids rushed into the emergency room wasn't her kid. Desiree stole from the house but Evelyn wouldn't change the lock. The door would be open whenever she came home. It was as bad as it had ever been.

Then things got worse after that.

One of her plugs got locked up. Another started cutting his pills with something cheaper—Desiree didn't know what it was, only that it burned her throat and made her black out for hours. She had bruises she couldn't explain.

She'd wake up in unfamiliar places, her backpack gone, her phone dead. Clothes dishevelled, sometimes off. Once, she found herself in a gas station bathroom with vomit on her shirt and a bloody nose.

She was only seventeen, but she felt thirty.

*****

"Ugh!" Desiree grunted when she woke up alone in an abandoned house. She sat up and tried to remember how she got here. Nothing came but she was happy to find herself fully dressed. She finally admitted defeat and decided to go home.

"Desiree?" Evelyn hoped when she heard the soft knocking on the door. Her mom opened the door slowly, lips tight, eyes unreadable.

"Please," Desiree whispered. "I just need to sleep."

Mrs. Carter didn't say anything. Just moved aside. Desiree walked in and collapsed on the couch. She curled into a ball and sobbed—deep, ugly sobs that shook her whole body. Her mother sat beside her but didn't touch her. She wanted to but the girl was so fragile she looked like she might break.

"I want to stop," Desiree choked out. "I swear I do. I just don' t know how."

"You need real help, baby. Not just rest." Evelyn managed. She found another rehabilitation center out in the mountains. The reviews were mixed but she would try.

"I' m scared." Desiree admitted. She had survived many close calls and lived through life-or-death situations. She had seen people hurt and killed in the streets.

"I am too." her mother moaned because she saw the bodies too. She saw the evil things people did to each other.

*****

They tried again. A new program with new counselors and new promises. Even a new Ms. Lena since another woman counselor took to the teen. Ms. Donna poured her heart and soul into the teen so she wouldn't end up on the wall. The entrance to the center was filled with pictures of the ones who didn't make it. Some looked just like Desiree.

She started off strong and even started drawing again. She sketched a portrait of Ms. Lena from memory and gave it to her in group. They hugged. It was the first time she' d been hugged by someone who didn' t want anything from her in months.

"I' m proud of you," Ms. Donna said and dropped a genuine tear.

"Me too!" Desiree smiled through her own tears. "I'm going to make it this time!"

"I know," Ms. Donna sighed. She hoped she would, believed she would.

Desiree started writing poems again. About pain. About

addiction. About trying to find her way back. She never gave testimonials before but read one of poems aloud in group and everyone clapped.

It felt like hope.

But hope is fragile. And temptation is patient. The devil is patient.

*****

"I'm going out..." Desiree decided and announced.

"Where? Why?" Evelyn demanded. She had been doing great since she came home and knew nothing was out there. Nothing good that is.

"Just need some air ma! Tired of being cooped up in the house!" she fussed. Her mother fussed back but couldn't physically stop her.

Desiree left the house in a storm of anger but swore to herself she wouldn' t use. She just needed air.

She ended up at the train station, where some old heads were hanging out. One of them recognized her.

"Dez, you looking skinny as hell. You good?" an old acquaintance asked.

"I' m fine." Desiree sighed. She had yet to regain the weight she lost and felt self conscious about it. Which was a good enough reason to want something to feel better. "Got anything?"

"I got something. Clean. Strong. No cap." the old friend declared and produced some pills.

Desiree hesitated as she faced her temptation face to face. All she had to do was reach out and take one but all the classes and meetings weighed on her mind.

'Just one more time,' she thought. 'Just to take the edge off.'

"New stuff!" He handed her two pills. Little white ones with a new stamp she hadn't seen before.

She didn't notice since she didn't even look before she swallowed one dry.

And never reached the second.

CHAPTER SEVEN:
Numb

The train station bathroom smelled like bleach, old piss, and cheap cologne. The mirror was cracked in three places. A single fluorescent light above the sink flickered on and off like it couldn' t make up its mind.

Desiree knew she was in trouble instantly. She was rising too far, too fast. Faster and further than ever before. Her chapped lips throbbed. Her pale skin hummed as if electric current flowed through it. Eyes open but she couldn't see. Then everything went blurry.

The first pill had kicked in and second was still in her palm. She managed to tuck it into a safe place as she slid down the wall, knees pulled to her chest. Everything felt slow. Distant like she was underwater, watching the world through a thick glass.

That's how the janitor found her, slumped behind the toilet. Barely breathing. Pulse faint. He'd seen it enough to know what he was seeing. Seen it enough to know what to do so he called 911.

"We got another kid overdosing!" he shouted. The urgency in his voice matched the age she appeared. The face was hardened but she still looked twelve to him.

Luckily Paramedics were close and arrived quick enough to spare her life. Narcan in both nostrils brought her back from the brink, just in the nick of time.

She woke up hours later in the ER, gasping like she' d been dragged back from the bottom of the ocean. Her mother stood over her looking like death herself. Eyes bloodshot. Hands clenched so tight her knuckles were white.

"Ma?" Desiree needed to ask because the room spun counterclockwise. Then stopped, shimmied and spun the other direction.

"You almost died, Desiree," she whispered.

"I didn' t mean to." Desiree apologized stared at the ceiling, blinking slowly.

"They never do." Her mother sighed and reached out and took her hand. For the first time in months, Desiree didn' t pull away. "I don' t want to lose you."

"I already feel lost," Desiree croaked, her throat raw.

"Then let' s find you. Together." her mother pleaded. They failed before but she would not give up. Another mother just said goodbye to her daughter's shell in this same room two hours before.

*****

That was the beginning of the third recovery. The third time was a charm so she was hopeful. This program was intensive, inpatient.

Thirty days. No phones. No visitors for the first week. Desiree hated every second of it. Hated the plastic mattress, the group exercises, the way people looked at her like a project instead of a person.

But slowly, she started talking. She eventually started listening. Most of all she started healing.

She met a girl named Aaliyah, seventeen, who overdosed

122

twice in one year. Aaliyah had track marks down her arms and a tattoo on her collarbone that said stay alive. They shared stories during group. Laughed when no one was looking. Cried when no one judged.

"You remind me of my little sister," Aaliyah said one night.

"I don' t even remind me of me," Desiree replied. That was the worst part, being a stranger to herself. She once apologized to a woman in the bathroom until she noticed it was her own reflection.

"You will! We're going to shake this thing together!" Aaliyah declared. "Accountability partners!"

"I like that!" Desiree nodded to the way it sounded.

"We can't punk out!" Aaliyah demanded with a smile.

"I ain't no punk," Desiree determined and puffed her chest.

"We call every day to make sure we're good. Then if we feel," Aaliyah said and paused to find the right word. "Uh crazy. Then we call each other again. Don't let me fall."

"I won't let you fall," Desiree assured. "Don't let me fall either!"

The new friends hugged like their lives depended on it. They kinda did since they vowed to keep each other alive. Something Aaliyah couldn't do for her sister. The one Desiree reminded her of.

*****

Desiree had a desire to live after the near-death experience. Actually was dead before the paramedics brought her back. Now she wanted to live. She wanted to draw again, write poems again. Death gave her life so she wrote about survival.

One of them was pinned to the wall of the art room before she left:

I was drowning in air,

calling out without sound.

But now I see the surface.

And I want to be found.

"Welcome back!" Miss Hunter cheered when her prized student finally returned. It was against the rules but she pulled the girl in and squeezed.

"Good to be back!" Desiree sighed and basked in her arms. She felt safe in her embrace, the streets not so much.

The hood was still moving at the speed of the hood when she got home but things felt different. The streets felt louder, faster. The nights colder, harder. Her old friends unreachable.

She texted Jade once.

'I'm good. Clean now. Hope you're okay too.'

No response so she didn't text again. Bree had immersed herself in the streets now so there was no need to reach out. Guilt and shame prevented her from texting Tati. The best she could muster was 'liking' her post, to show she was watching.

As promised she and Aaliyah texted daily. The first of the day was their accountability pact. The other twenty or thirty because they were friends. She had fallen so far behind in school she enrolled in online classes to catch up.

She tried to eat right. Sleep on schedule. Do small things like clean her room and brush her teeth before noon. It was hard. Some days harder than others. But she was trying. She wanted to live.

Evelyn was trying too and worked every shift she could manage. The hood was a part of the problem so she was determined to move her daughter away from the hood. To suburbs where people didn't hang out in the streets all night. Dealers didn't lurk on every corner. She treated enough people from the suburbs with drug overdoses to know it wasn't immune. It wasn't just in your face on every corner either. Because no matter where you go you bring you with you.

*****

Then came the funerals. The first was Malik. They saw each other in passing but kept walking since there wasn't anything to talk about anymore. She not only regretted the time they spent but resented him for turning her onto the deadly addiction.

He was found bloated in his sparse apartment. Word spread fast that he'd taken something laced. Same corner, same story. Only this time, no one found him in time. Evelyn forced her to attend because she needed to see. Needed to see the boy she thought she loved. Needed to hear the moans and walls of his mother and grandmother, sisters and brothers.

Desiree didn't cry at first. Maybe because he looked nothing like he looked in life. She didn't hear a word the preacher said until the casket was finally lowered into the ground. Aaliyah texted to make sure she was ok but she wasn't. She didn't text back and just sat on her porch, watching the clouds pass overhead like nothing had changed.

But everything had because that night, she relapsed. She didn't mean to. It wasn't even pills this time.

Just weed. A few puffs and a pass with a friend in passing. There was no need to bother Aaliyah with that so she didn't text.

The next time either since it was just alcohol. After what she had been through she needed a drink. Which is the crazy things alcoholics say because no one ever actually needed a drink. People need to not drink so they don't add problems to whatever problems they were trying to escape. Drugs and alcohol don't help problems, they multiply them.

"Sup you," Bree asked when she spotted Desiree on the front porch. She rarely ventured beyond it since returning home from her latest stint at rehab. It should have been her safe space while her mother worked double shifts to get them out of the hood. But it was still in the hood and wasn't safe.

"Hey," Desiree sighed deeply and kept her vigil over the hood.

"Messed up about Jessie..." Bree sighed as well for the latest of their classmates to succumb to the hood. The hood could and would kill you in many ways and he was the latest to fall victim to the plague of gun violence.

"Yeah," she replied because it was messed up. Her shoulders still shrugged because they were becoming desensitized to death. No kid should shrug their shoulders at death. Inner cities were more dangerous as third world, war torn countries.

"Here..." Bree offered and extended her hand. "Just something to mellow out."

Desiree studied the pill for an eternity as all the lessons, mottos and mantras of rehab came to mind. Clips of the different testimonials crossed her mind. Aaliyah's number echoed in her head. Still she reached for the pill. It would be her last.

Desiree popped the pill with the juice she had been nursing for an hour. The effects came soon after as the pill dissolved in her stomach and dispersed into her system. Her vision blurred, hearing dimmed. She didn't even notice when Bree took her leave and hopped into a car with a couple of guys. For a split second, she felt

126

her body float again. And in that second, she knew this time might be the last time.

*****

But it wasn' t. She woke up the next morning, alive. Sick, disgusted with herself but alive. Ashamed, but alive, and both were good.

Aaliyah had texted again but she didn't text back. Instead she called and her friend answered immediately.

"You good?" Aaliyah asked even though she knew she wasn't. She knew she fell off the wagon when she didn't return the last series of text.

"Hi," she whispered.

"You okay?" her friend asked again. Softly, no judgement, just concern.

"No," Desiree replied. "But I want to be."

"Meet me at S&S. Chicken and waffles on me!" Aaliyah cheered.

"Yeah ok," Desiree said and knocked away a tear. She knew she could never beat this alone. Thanks to her real friend she wouldn't have to.

CHAPTER EIGHT:
False Hope

"We made it!" Evelyn cheered to no one as she spun around in the new kitchen of the new house. They indeed made it and moved out to the suburbs. But wherever you go you bring yourself with you.

"Sure did!" Desiree sang as she joined her in the kitchen. It took more than she knew she had in her to make it this far. It takes a village to raise a child but even more support to heal a junkie. Some never heal, just don't use.

Desiree had ups and down as she fell off the wagon a few times. Ms Lena, Ms Donna and Aaliyah all pitched in and helped her climb back up on the wagon. They refused to give up and she made it out. A new house, new school, new life.

"Well, let me get out of here," Evelyn announced after a beep on her watch said it was time to go to work. Work was at the fancy new hospital out here in the suburbs as well.

She didn't have the same sense of dread about going to work. She signed up to be a nurse to help people but what she saw in the hood almost made her get a truck and deliver Amazon. The hood emergency room was like on the front lines of a battle field. Seeing the broken bodies and horrible things people did to her made her sick.

The suburbs weren't without problems since there were just as many overdoses here than there. Which didn't surprise her since half the drug overdoses back in the old hospital came from these upscale zip codes. The only difference here was the violence.

"Thanks again ma," Desiree sighed. She and Evelyn locked eyes as smiled.

"You're welcome dear," she quickly responded since she knew what she was thanking her for. For saving her life. "My pleasure!"

The sun felt different that spring. It was warmer, softer—like the world had been holding its breath and finally exhaled. Desiree sat on the back steps of her house, sipping tea, wrapped in her mother's old robe. Her curls were tied up, her skin beginning to clear, and her eyes—while still shadowed—held something new.

A flicker of fight.

*****

Senior year, new school and Desiree had started over. Again. She was in new group with a new sponsor. She still had Ms. Lena who wasn't just a counselor, she was her lifeline. Desiree called her every morning. At first to check in, eventually just to talk. About art. About music. About everything except pills and pain.

"You gotta give the good parts of yourself as much attention as the bad," Ms. Lena told her one day.

"I am!" Desiree agreed, and did.

She still texted Aaliyah each morning, even after the line was disconnected. The new owner of the line asked her to stop so she had their conversations in her mind. Pretending that her friend was there was better than the grim reality. Aaliyah occasionally slipped from the wagon. She too always made it back up. Until one time she didn't.

Desiree was enjoying the freedoms that came from moving away from the hood. She even got a new used car when she got her license. Driving to school sure beat the crowded, noisy, dangerous public buses she took back and forth to school in the hood.

She didn't have much in common with the kids at the new school but was well liked. Even more important she painted again. Slowly, cautiously and thoughtful. Her first piece was small—a broken clock melting over the edge of a windowsill. Ms. Lena asked what it meant.

"Time feels fake now," Desiree said. "Like I lost years, and I can' t get them back."

"But you' re still here," Ms. Lena reminded her. "Time ain' t up."

"I know but," Desiree began but paused since she never admitted this out loud. "I just feel like I'm on borrowed time."

*****

She got a part-time job at a small art supply store. Minimum wage, but it came with peace. The smell of paint. The feel of paper. The quiet buzz of fluorescent lights and jazz music playing through the speakers. One day, her boss—a retired painter named Mr. Jordan—gave her an old sketchbook.

"You got the kind of pain that turns into beauty if you let it," he said.

"Yeah," she agreed since she saw the pain in her own eyes in the mirror.

Desiree took it home and started filling the pages. Lines turned into figures. Shadows into emotion. Her trauma started taking shape—one stroke at a time. There was still something left to do so she grabbed her phone and did it.

*****

"Hello!" a voiced barked at the new number on her phone screen. The hostility in the tone made Desiree smile.

"Hey girl. It's me," she said and heard a smile come through the line.

"Desiree? That's you!" Tati exclaimed.

"Yeah. It's me and I just wanted to apologize for..." Desiree said as she rehearsed.

"Don't be sorry to me!" Tati shot back. That ghetto girl spunk made her laugh since Tati was still one of the smartest people she knew. Her tone went somber when she revealed. "I thought you were gonna die,"

"I did," Desiree confessed. She actually ODed twice but was in the right place at the right time and was saved.

"But you didn't!" Tati shouted back. "Bree gone. Malik gone, Ray, Julia..."

Desiree blinked and blanked out at the long list of fallen soldiers from their old hood. It sounded like a general announcing the fallen troops after a hard fought battle. Except these were all kids from their school.

"When the last time you been to S&S?" Desiree cut in on the obituary. They used to take the train and bus away from the hood to eat at their favorite chicken and waffle spot.

"Not since you left," Tati admitted and pouted.

"Meet me their Saturday!" she blurted. It was out now so she ran with it.

"Bet!" Tati happily agreed. They cut the call to pick up when

131

they saw each other.

They met up at a diner and split fries like they used to, both of them changed, but somehow still themselves. They didn' t cry. They just held hands across the sticky table and let the silence say the rest. No more talk of the dead, just plans for living over their favorite food.

"Awe man!" Tati groaned when rain began to pelt the window over dessert.

"Don't worry, I'll drop you," Desiree offered since she knew how long it took Tati to get her hair like that. She had opted for ponytails these days but appreciated her friend's hairdo.

"You for real!" Tati cheered. She was so excited her friend was sure now.

"Yeah. I got you girl," she agreed. She owed her for being a friend.

"Thought you would never come back here," Tati broke the silence when the view went from chic to bleak.

"Yeah..." Desiree whispered as she took it all in. She couldn't understand how people could live like this after seeing life if the burbs. She decided then she would never come back. She could never come back.

*****

But she did. Desiree and Tati spoke daily and laughed about their classmates to each other. Busy schedules prevented them from linking up again but the old friends were friends again. A few weeks later Desiree received an invitation to the hood.

Ms. Lena was hosting an event and wanted her star poet to come grace the place with her face. Desiree didn't hesitate to agree to help the woman who helped her so much. She spent the next few days writing different pieces but they all ended up in the trash can.

Mr. Jordan had encouraged her to paint from her heart and she was producing gallery worthy pieces. She decided to take the same approach with the poem and put the pen down. She had lived three lifetimes in her seventeen years. More than enough pain to produce a poem.

She invited Tati and secretly hoped Aaliyah would magically appear. Tati couldn't get off work because she needed every penny her piece of a job could produce. Her mother was third generation public assistance so she would have to get herself out of the hood. She would not be the fourth generation.

Saturday morning and Desiree presented a poem and painting together at a community open mic hosting a recovery celebration. She remembered quite a few faces from her different stints at rehab. Some she didn't recognize since they didn't look the same anymore.

Her voice shook at first, then steadied when she remembered who she was. Desiree Carter and she was born for this.

She read:

In shadows deep, Desiree Carter stands,

With whispered dreams woven through her hands.

I died a few times, yet the dawn still gleams,

A phoenix rising from the ashes of dreams.

In the tapestry of life, I thread my heart,

Each scar a story, each heartbeat a part.

Through trials faced and the love I've given,

I'm woven into the fabric of living.

The room went quiet at first as the listeners processed what they just listened to. Wide eyes blinked at the reality that was once them too. The poem wasn't about her, it was about them too. Ms. Lena was the first to clap from the poem that left Desiree winded.

The room clapped slowly as people stood one by one. Soon every seat was empty as hands pounded together in applause. Some cried but not from sorry. It was relief, relief they made it. It was at that moment Desiree knew what she wanted to do with her life.

She wanted to help others climb out too.

*****

Desiree didn't think or dare even blink as she drove along on her mission. She told no one about it because they would all try and talk her out of it. And would succeed since it was ill advised. Still, she needed to do it. She lifted her chin above the hood and came to a stop where it all started.

She ignored the noise and climbed the steps to the raggedy home. It seemed even more rundown after living on a block of well maintained homes with manicured lawns. All the cars shined from the weekly washes in the driveway that was a ritual in the suburbs.

"You got a dollar?" a kid demanded as she snatched open the door.

"A dollar..." Desiree asked and began to pull her purse around.

"Can I get a twenty?" a woman asked as she appeared behind the child. Desiree recognized her as one of Jade's aunts and tucked her purse.

"I don't have any money," she declined and got down to what she came for. "Where's Jade?"

"How anyone supposed to know that?" her aunt laughed and walked away.

"She not here," the little girl announced.

Desiree was almost relieved her old friend wasn't home. She second-guessed her decision to come here and help. Now it was time to drive back to the burbs and continue working on herself. Jade appeared on the next block waving at cars and dancing in the street.

'Just keep going,' Desiree heard in her mind but shook it away.

"Ms. Lena didn't just leave me," she said out loud and pulled over to the curb.

"You got a few dollars I can get..." Jade asked for the hundredth time today. The words were still in the air as her war torn mind processed the face. "Tati? No, no, um...Desiree!"

"Yeah girl. Get in. Let's get something to eat," she sighed and popped the locks.

"You driving now!" Jade asked like it was a strange thing. Driving was just a right of passage where she lived now. Her new school had a student parking lot since most kids drove once they were old enough.

"Huh?" Desiree asked although she heard the words clearly. What confused her was how the girl looked. Jade was once the baddest chick in the school. Finest too but now she skinny, sweaty with a dank odor. She looked like a shadow of the girl she used to be.

"Dez···" she said, swaying slightly. "It's rough out

here."

"I know. That's why I'm here. Here to help," she said and steered towards their destination.

"Where are we going?" Jade asked when it was obvious they were leaving their immediate hood. Most hood people liked to stay in their own particular hood. The devil they knew...

"To First Steps rehabilitation clinic. Ms Donna has a program for..." she was saying before Jade cut in.

"I'm not a junky! I don't need no rehab!" she insisted. "I was about to quit anyway! I got this!"

"Jade, they can help you. They helped me," she assured but her old friend wouldn't hear it.

"You can just take me home. I'm good," Jade said and gripped the door handle.

"Ok. I'm just trying to help," Desiree moaned. One concept from her stints in rehab came to mind since you can't help anyone who doesn't want to be helped.

"I know. I appreciate it," Jade said sincerely. It just wasn't her time and she wasn't ready. "Ooh! There's José! Stop!"

"Who? Huh?" Desiree asked and came to an urgent stop. Jade hopped out before she could come to a complete stop and ran over the the man. She was ready to pull away but Jade rushed back and hopped inside. "I know you didn't just cop something!"

"Huh?" she asked since she did.

"Yeah, yeah. Just need a chill." Jade smiled. "Wanna split it?"

Desiree stared at the pill in her friend's hand and blinked. A rush of emotions flooded her senses and she could almost feel the warm opiate rush in her system. It was so small. So familiar.

What could half a pill hurt. You have been doing so good! A treat! Reward yourself...

'NO!' Her mind screamed silently to drown out the devil's whispers. But her heart whispered, Don't. Even when jade snapped the pill in half and extended.

"Nah. I'm good," Desiree croaked and looked away. This was where she came from and she wasn't going back. Jade popped the pill and hopped out of the car.

Desiree pulled away and didn't look back. That night, she cried harder than she had in months. Not because she was strong. She realized just how weak she really was.

CHAPTER NINE:
The Last High

Desiree hadn' t felt this strong in a long time. 189 days to be exact since her last relapse. Over six months of clean time, marked quietly in the back of her sketchbook. She didn' t post about it. Didn' t brag. She knew how fragile sobriety could be—how fast the bottom could fall out.

Still, something inside her had shifted.

She was working two days a week at the art store now. Studying online. Rebuilding trust with her mom, brick by brick. Her art had even been accepted into a small community gallery showcase. For the first time in forever, Desiree could see a future—and it didn' t terrify her.

Finals were aced and graduation was near. She made it but so many of her old friends did not. Of the old crew only she and Tati would graduate from high school. They congratulated each other on the phone but Desiree had her fill of the hood and vowed to never step foot back in it.

By the end of the school year both Tati and Desiree augmented their friendship with new friends. No one that could take the place of fill the space of the years they spent growing up. Just the day to day faces around them in school.

For Desiree it was Kacie from art class. They bonded over pieces and soon texted, talked and hung out together. Kacie was born and raised in this suburban utopia. As such she was amazed at Desiree's hood upbringing.

Desiree thought it was cute and didn't mind being her ghetto tour guide from the safety of the suburbs. She taught her the latest dances and slang words. Even braided her Caucasian hair in corn rows.

It was on the strength of their friendship Desiree agreed to attend the end of the year party. It was the stuff of legend freshmen heard about when they finally reached high school. They waited patiently until their turn came in four years and now it was time.

"What do you wear to a suburban party?" Desiree quipped as she tried on outfits. She much preferred the dress code out here than the city. Slut rap had infected the hood and had girls and teens dressing like mini prostitutes. Dancing like them too.

"That's fine!" Kacie nodded at the dress Desiree held up to herself.

"Cuz it matches yours!" she laughed and stepped into the attached bathroom to change.

"Nice!" Kacie cheered when she returned. The dresses were long enough to be classy but still showed off their shapes. "Let's go turn on!"

"Up. Turn up!" Desiree laughed and school her head. They got a good laugh and headed out of the house.

"Have fun guys!" Evelyn called after them as they left the house. She was getting ready to catch another shift since mortgage was different from rent. The overnight shift in the suburbs was easy money since nothing much ever happened. Not like back in Philly where kids shot each other with machine guns.

"We will!" the girls called back as one. Kacie drove over so they decided to ride in her car for the evening.

"This is gonna be, lit?" Kacie asked cautiously and got the

nod from Desiree.

"All the way up!" Desiree cheered.

The party lived up to the hype from the moment they walked inside. The music was pumping the latest jams and kids packed the dance floor. This was nothing like a party in the hood since no one was fighting. No opps shooting at each other with machine guns either. A lot of drugs and alcohol though, just like the hood.

"No, we don't..." Desiree tried to decline when someone made a drive-by drink delivery and placed beers in both hands.

"One won't hurt," Kacie shrugged and took a sip. She had been waiting four years for this party so she decided to party.

"Yeah?" Desiree asked because she wasn't so sure. She didn't want to poop the party so she took a sip and slipped from the band wagon once more.

By the third beer they had taken over the dance floor. Their new dance moves made them the life of the party and all eyes were on them. The boys too came bearing gifts. Each offered a beer, a joint and finally a pill.

"Want to?" Kacie asked wide eyed as she produced the two pills. Desiree knew exactly what they were and what they did and shook her head.

"We better not," she sighed. They shared a lot but she never told her about the addition that nearly claimed her life more than once.

"Everyone is doing it!" Kacie said and looked around the room. "I never tried it before."

"So why start now," Desiree reasoned.

"Because it's a party! The last party of high school! Then off

140

to college!" she explained. "Please! With me!"

"Oh, ok," Desiree caved under the pressure from her peer. Life is all about the choices we make and they chose to pop the pills and swallow them with their beer. That was the last thing she ever remembered.

*****

"Look alive! Mass casualties in route!" a voice blared through the intercom at 2:16 a.m. "Paramedics were called to a house on Washington circle."

"Here we go!" Evelyn sighed and got prepped. So many parties got shot up back home she was ready to save some lives. Except this wasn't gunfire to contend with.

"We got several overdoses! Get narcam, IV drips..." the doctor relayed as the first of several ambulances began to arrive. They skidded to a stop and downloaded the dying kids.

The nurses and doctors sprang into action to save lives. A couple more ambulances pulled up with less urgency since it was too late for them.

"Oh no!" Evelyn moaned when she saw Kacie on the gurney. The blue lips and foam from her nostrils pronounced her dead before the doctor did. "Where's Desiree! Where's my daughter!"

Evelyn pulled her cell phone and began speed dialing her daughter. The calls went straight to voicemail so she kept trying. The last time she called coincided with the next ambulance door open and the familiar ring tone.

"She coded," a paramedic sighed in utter defeat of the teenage girls on the gurney. "Looks like fentanyl"

At 2:22 a.m., Desiree Carter was pronounced dead at Grady Memorial Hospital. The same place she was born seventeen years before.

"At least you can finally rest. Rest baby," Evelyn whispered as if she might wake her. She had felt like they were on borrowed time since the first overdose. Now that time had run its course.

CHAPTER TEN:
What She Left Behind

The church was full was full even though they hadn't live out here for long. Long enough for everyone who ever met Desiree Carter come to see her off. There was nine funerals that week and all filled to capacity.

Not just the new ones because the hood showed up to see her off as well. The tears flowed from broken hearted Old teachers. Classmates. Distant cousins. People from her mother' s job. Tati sat in the front pew, face pale, hands shaking. Ms. Lena was beside her, shoulders firm but eyes wet. The art store owner, Mr. Jordan, wore a tie for the first time in a decade.

And at the center of it all, a closed casket.

The pastor didn't know her so he read from the paper, "Desiree Carter. Gone at seventeen. A life that had barely begun. A soul that had burned too bright, too fast."

The pastor spoke gently, trying to balance sorrow and grace. He talked about struggle. About the silent wars young people fight. About how pain wears many faces. About how addiction wasn' t a choice, but the result of too many wrong ones.

Mrs. Carter didn' t speak but she had no choice. The words weren't her own since she found Desiree's handwritten eulogy in daughter' s sketchbook

She couldn' t speak so she let her daughter speak for herself.

If you' re reading this, I' m sorry.

I tried. God knows, I tried.

I wanted to be free

But I didn't know how.

I wanted to live

But I couldn't face now.

Tell the ones who come after me:

Life is about choices

Please choose different.

Please choose you.

The room fell silent. A collective ache spread through every chest. And for the first time since Desiree's passing, her mother let herself cry. Now that is was over. Now that it was

The End

Aftermath

A week later, a small art exhibit opened in the library downtown. It was called "Choices: The Art & Words of Desiree Carter."

The pieces told the story she couldn't say out loud: A watercolor of a girl in a hoodie surrounded by shadows labeled pressure, doubt, and loneliness

A sketch of pills falling like rain over a wilted flower

A poem titled "Highs & Goodbyes" written in jagged ink

And finally, a bright acrylic painting of a rising sun breaking through a cracked window, titled Hope Lives Here.

The exhibit was visited by hundreds. Teachers brought students. Counselors brought clients. Mothers brought daughters.

Some left in tears, most left inspired. But no one left unchanged.

Tati started volunteering with a youth recovery program.

Ms. Lena launched a nonprofit called "Desiree's Voice" – focused on mental health, addiction prevention, and creative therapy for teens.

Even Jade–still in recovery–showed up at the ribbon-cutting, eyes clear for the first time in years.

Desiree's death was a tragedy. But it wasn't the end of her

story. She had left behind more than pain.

She had left behind a warning. A message. A legacy of choice.

And in the quiet of a thousand hearts, her voice still whispered:

Choose love.

Choose light.

Choose life.

Author's Note:
A Real Choice

Desiree's story is fiction.

But what she went through is not.

Every day in America, more than 290 families lose someone to a drug overdose.

In 2023 alone, over 105,000 people died — and nearly 80,000 of them involved opioids, mostly fentanyl. Many of those who died weren't long-time users. They were first-timers, or people who thought they were taking something else. One pill. One hit. One moment that couldn't be undone.

Fentanyl is fifty times stronger than heroin and often hidden in pills that look safe.

There's no way to see it, smell it, or taste it — until it's too late.

If you or someone you love is struggling with addiction, please know this:

Help exists. Recovery is real. You are not alone.

National Helpline (SAMHSA): 1-800-662-HELP (4357)

Free, confidential support — 24 hours a day, every day.

Or visit findtreatment.gov for local options.

We can't rewrite the past, but we can choose the next page.

Every day we wake up is another chance to choose life, to reach out, to begin again.

Desiree's story ends with survival — let yours begin there.